The Elevator Kiss

AMINA THULA

This edition published in 2015 by Ankara Press

© Amina Thula, 2014
© Cover Print design Vlisco

All rights reserved. The whole of this work is protected by copyright. No parts of this work may be loaded, stored, manipulated, reproduced or transmitted in any form or by any means, electronic or mechanical, including photocopying and recording, or by any information, storage and retrieval system without prior written permission from the publisher, on behalf of the copyright owner.
A catalogue record for this book is available from the Nigerian National Library.

ISBN: 978-978-53151-6-5

Editor: Anthea Gordon
Production and layout: Jibril Lawal
Cover design art: Onyinye Iwu

Ankara Press:
62B, Arts and Crafts Village
Opposite Sheraton, Abuja, Nigeria
www.ankarapress.com

One

Deck the halls with boughs of holly,
Fa la la la la, la la la la.
'Tis the season to be jolly,
Fa la la la la, la la la la.

The soft sounds of the Christmas carol greeted Sindi as she entered the plush lobby of Boateng Towers. It was her first time visiting Lulu, her best friend from university, in her new home. The interior of the building was even more impressive than the exterior. The floors were made of diamond-patterned marble and big off-white marble pillars divided the foyer into three sections. To the right of the entrance lay a bar. Beyond the bar was a grand door with frosted glass, which led to what looked like a restaurant. The middle section directly ahead of her served as the reception area and a huge Christmas tree sat right in the middle of the foyer. Two uniformed receptionists sat behind an imposing dark-wood desk. The last section, to the left, was the lounge area; a baby grand piano sat nestled amongst luxurious leather couches, end tables and coffee tables. Sindi walked over to the receptionists.

"Hello," she greeted the two ladies with a smile.

"Good day, ma'am," they both responded, smiling.

"I'm here to visit Luyanda Kente in apartment 102. I'm Sindiswa Mali."

One of the receptionists discreetly spoke into her intercom phone, then pushed her chair back and stood up.

"Please follow me," she said, making her way to an elevator next to the reception desk, where she punched a code into the keypad. "When the elevator arrives press F6. The apartment numbers are written on the doors."

Sindi smiled her thanks. The receptionist turned and made her way back to the reception desk.

Christmas Day. Another year gone by. Sindi's hand tapped her clutch bag against her legs as she reflected on the passing year while she waited for the elevator. *What a year it has been*; it felt like she had gone through 12 years in 12 months. She still couldn't believe her fiancé's betrayal – *ex*-fiancé – she corrected herself. Mandla and Sindi had been partners in a small but very successful events management and catering company, which had held an impressive list of clients. Their relationship had seemed solid and they'd been set to get married on the previous New Year's Eve – Mandla's idea. He had told her he could think of nothing better than welcoming the New Year together as Mr and Mrs Mandla Silo. Sindi had agreed just to please him. She would have much preferred a smaller and more intimate ceremony to the extravagant wedding he had planned. But as with most aspects of their relationship in the past couple of years she went along with him in order to keep the peace. So the humiliation was that much greater when, instead of showing up at the wedding, Mandla had sent her a text message minutes before she was due to walk down the aisle, breaking up with her and leaving her to deal with the guests and the expenses. A week later when she had found the strength to return to work she'd learned that, not only had Mandla squandered all the money in their business and most of the savings in their joint account, but he had left her for some young Jo'burg fly girl. She was broke, owed a lot of people a lot of money and her personal assets were to be attached as the business was in her name. Her body had gone into complete shock; she had landed in hospital for two weeks.

That was then, this is now. I'm too strong to break over Mandla. This is just a temporary situation. I was a success before and I will be again. After all, I'm the one who started the company; he just joined an already successful venture.

The elevator pinged and the doors slid open. As she stepped into the elevator she started back in surprise. For a moment she stood rooted to the spot. She stared dumbly at the handsome man lounging with lazy confidence at the back of the elevator. He was tall, broad-shouldered and had a strong, lean body. The strength in his body was also etched in his face. *If Adonis had been a black man, this is what he would have looked like.* Sindi silently admired his face: big dark eyes, thick brows, strong nose and full, juicy lips. He cocked his head at her.

"Going up?" he asked in a baritone that made her ears ring. His voice reminded her of whisky; it had the same richness as the colour, the same smoothness as the liquid and it invoked the warmth of a mouthful. The fog that had settled over her mind slowly lifted as each word punctured her brain and was deciphered.

"Y-yes, sorry," she stammered as she stepped into the elevator. "I was just surprised to see you there – I didn't expect the elevator to be occupied."

She moved to the number pad but saw F6 had been pressed already. She also noted there was a parking floor. *That must be where he caught the elevator.* She gave him a small smile before she settled herself in the opposite corner. Beneath her eyelashes she studied him further. He was groomed like an African-American: his hair was closely shaven and the hairline was defined. He was wearing an expensive-looking, tailored, navy-blue cotton suit that fitted his figure to perfection. Underneath he had a navy-blue shirt on; the top buttons were unbuttoned, giving Sindi a sneak peek of his firm cocoa chest. Her eyes continued to rove over him, taking in every inch of his masculine physique. Suddenly their gazes collided. Feeling embarrassed and unsure if he knew she had been checking him out, Sindi shot him another quick smile before averting her eyes to the elevator doors. She could feel heat creeping up the back of her neck and over her ears to her face. *Thank God he can't see me blushing.*

Edward smiled. He had been performing the exact same exercise but, unlike her, he was more brazen about it. His interest had been piqued from the moment the elevator doors had slid open to reveal Sindi standing there looking elegant and sexy. His gaze travelled appreciatively from her face to her feet, and then back up again. She was tall, almost as tall as him. Her long, thick weave was slicked back and fell just below her shoulder blades, with an ever-so-tiny pouf sticking out in the front. Her eyes were almond-shaped and had a rich warm-brown colour that contrasted perfectly with her dark caramel complexion. There was something quite unsettling about her eyes though that he couldn't quite put his finger on. She was wearing a midnight-blue three-quarter sleeved figure-hugging boat-necked dress that ended just below her knees. Her jewellery consisted of a pair of gold statement earrings and a plain gold cuff bracelet on her wrist. She was holding an A4 envelope-sized bag: Chanel. He'd recognise it anywhere; after all he had bought one just like it for his sister as an early graduation gift last year. His gaze travelled even further down. The length of her dress emphasised her well-muscled calves, which were supported by strong, sexy ankles. The black high-heeled sandals on her pedicured feet framed her ankles to advantage. Her body was evenly proportioned and average sized and her round curves highlighted her luscious, soft femininity. Edward felt a strong desire to engage with her.

"Merry Christmas," he said breaking their silence.

Still feeling embarrassed, she shot him a quick glance that avoided meeting his eyes.

"Thank you," she replied with another small smile. "Merry Christmas to you too."

"Nice bag. My sister has one just like it."

"Thank you. I guess your sister has good taste."

"So do you, obviously," he laughed.

Sindi smiled at him, giving him confidence to carry on chatting with her.

"I thought I knew all my neighbours but I don't believe I have seen you around before; have you just moved in recently?"

"No, I'm visiting a friend."

"I'm Edward by the way," he said, extending his hand.

"Sindi," she responded, accepting his hand.

An unexpected surge of electricity coursed through them, causing them both to break the contact in shock. They stared at each other, stunned by what had just happened. The elevator pinged, breaking their reverie, and the doors slowly parted. Edward straightened up, pulling his jacket into place. He walked to the doors and held them open for Sindi.

"Thank you," she paused to say as she passed him.

She had hardly stepped into the entrance hall when four teenagers descended upon her, blocking her way.

"Wait!" one of the girls shrieked out. "You have to kiss!"

Startled and irrationally feeling guilty that her attraction to Edward had been busted, Sindi's defences went up. "Excuse me?"

"You two were standing under the mistletoe," the blonde girl explained, pointing to the decoration hanging above the elevator door.

Sindi looked up. "Oh-um ... No. I don't think so."

She attempted to walk past the teenagers but the four blocked her way again.

"You have to, it's tradition," the other girl, also with blonde hair, insisted.

"No ... I don't think so," Sindi repeated, trying to get past them again.

"Where's your Christmas spirit? Come on," one of the boys coaxed.

Sindi snapped. "I said no! And I *don't* have to do anything!"

The four young faces quickly sobered up with embarrassment. Sindi immediately regretted her harsh response. Spotting an opportunity, Edward decided to maximise on it. He walked over to Sindi to join in on the coaxing. He lightly touched her back. The intimate touch caused her to jump a little.

"Come on, Sindi, it's tradition. You can't say no. I can guarantee you: kissing me won't be an awful exercise," he said, his breath fanning her ear.

No. That rich voice of yours is what I can't say no to. Worn down by temptation and the challenge in Edward's voice, Sindi relented.

"I'm sorry, I didn't mean to snap at you," she apologised to the four teenagers. "You just caught me off-guard ... then you were so insistent ... I'll do it, I'll kiss him."

The teenagers cheered but they were less enthusiastic than when the elevator opened. Taking a deep breath she turned to face Edward. Sindi closed her eyes and tilted her face to his. Her lips puckered up to him with a mixture of anticipation and trepidation. Edward's hand slithered down to the small of her back and pulled her against him. His other hand moved under her hair to the base of her neck to support her head, causing her to tilt her head further. She caught a whiff of his cologne. The spicy masculine scent combined with his virility gave her an immediate head rush. His manhood pressed against her lower abdomen, creating all sorts of delicious somersaults. Heedlessly, she placed her hands on his hips and pulled him even closer. A smile played over his face as his lips lowered to meet hers but instead of kissing her he paused, his breath on her lips. Her lips parted as her heart rate picked up and her breath quickened. She breathed in his fresh minty breath. It played further havoc with her body. Her body became thoroughly wired as all her senses spiked up. *This must be how your senses feel when you first become blind and all the other senses are heightened.* Sindi lost awareness of her surroundings as her senses focused squarely on Edward. Her lips tingled as a soft, warm pressure pushed against them. His lips felt firm but gentle. Her mind exploded. His kiss started off tentative and slow, as if he was testing the waters, gauging how daring he could be. Slowly the kiss deepened, growing more fervent and confident. Her arms snaked around his waist, trying to pull him closer, even though it was impossible for them to be any closer than they already were. The move prompted him to tilt her head more, deepening their kiss further. Together they delved into the kiss, enjoying every moment. Seconds, minutes, hours. Time passed ... how much she didn't know ... all she knew was that she didn't want the kiss to end. Then suddenly she felt her right breast vibrate. Reluctantly, Edward broke their contact and fished his phone out of his inside jacket.

He turned away from her abruptly. "Yes!" he shouted into the phone.

A deep sense of isolation hit Sindi where his warm body had just been. Awareness of her surroundings returned as cool air hit her. As if from a distance she heard the teenagers' hooting and cheering as they climbed into the elevator. Shame washed over her at the realisation of what had just transpired. Embarrassed by her wanton response to a *stranger's* kiss in front of an *audience*, Sindi practically ran down the hall, desperate to reach the safety of Lulu's apartment. She found the apartment with ease, disregarded etiquette and rushed through the double doors without knocking. Sindi leaned against the door as she attempted to gather her wits and calm her pulsating heart. She lifted a shaky hand and smoothed it over her hair as she absorbed her surroundings.

The apartment was situated right at the marina. It was expansive and open-plan with fantastic views of the V&A Waterfront and Table Mountain. In the background she could hear Luther Vandross singing something about being in love and Christmas. Lulu's apartment was tastefully furnished in creams, beiges and touches of turquoise, the apartment fitted perfectly into its setting. Everything about the apartment spoke of style, glamour and class – not that she expected anything less from Lulu. She could see guests milling about on the sweeping balcony outside. When she felt she had gathered enough composure she pushed herself away from the door and made her way towards the other guests. She nearly bumped into Lulu who was coming out of the kitchen carrying a tray of hors d'oeuvres. Lulu's face broke into delighted smile.

"Sindi!" she exclaimed, welcoming Sindi with a kiss on the cheek.

Lulu looked every bit the lady of the manor in her sea-green floor-length Grecian-inspired billowing dress, her Brazilian weave cascading down her shoulders in flirtatious curls. "I'm so happy you could make it! Come, let me introduce you to everyone. We're waiting for one more guest to arrive, then we can sit down for our Christmas lunch. I just spoke to him; he should be here any moment."

"Oh wait, before we go outside I have something for you," Sindi said, pulling a small gift out of her clutch.

"Oh, friend … you didn't have to," Lulu said, placing the tray in her hand on the nearby console table. Lulu accepted the tiny gift box and opened it with the excitement of a six-year-old on Christmas morning.

"Tickets to the Selaelo Selota and Friends concert! Yay!" she squealed. "I thought the tickets were sold out? Thank you!"

"It's not much, but I wanted to thank you for all the help and support you've given me, not just this year, but throughout our friendship."

"Oh, please. You know you would have done the exact same thing for me and, besides, you've supported and helped me just as much over the years," Lulu said, giving Sindi a tight hug. Picking up the tray again she said with a smile, "Come let's go join the others before we get all soppy and ruin our mascara."

Sindi started to follow Lulu to the balcony when the doorbell rang.

"Will you get that for me please?" Lulu asked with a mischievous glint in her eyes. Sindi noticed the look with suspicion but decided to let it go and went to open the door.

Two

Her eyes widened in surprise when she swung the door open. Her first instinct was to slam it shut but his quick reaction stopped her. *Someone out there really has it in for me this year*, she thought as her heart rate picked up.

Edward smiled lazily and leaned his tall body against the door frame. He pushed his hands into his trouser pockets.

"I wondered where you'd scurried off to," he drawled as he cocked his head to the side.

Sindi lifted an eyebrow. "Scurried? Your choice of word implies I ran away scared."

"Well, didn't you?"

"No," she said, before turning and walking away.

The lazy smile on Edward's lips turned into one of amusement. With a swift move he strode in front of her and blocked her way. He inched closer to her. His gaze dropped to her lips. His scent ignited her senses once more. The memory of the kiss they had shared just moments ago seared her mind. Her instincts screamed for her to move away but she fought the urge, not willing to give him the satisfaction of knowing how he affected her.

"Then why did you disappear?"

His face was far, *far* too close to hers. Mint breath, lazy baritone – she was unable to maintain her composure any longer. She walked around him towards the party with all the false nonchalance she could muster.

"I had an engagement to attend," she threw over her shoulder as she stalked off to the balcony with as much equilibrium as her jelly legs would allow.

Edward watched her with amusement as she sashayed away. He wondered if she was aware of the inviting swing in her hips when she walked or how seductive it was. He was oh so glad he had chosen Lulu's invitation over spending the holidays with his family. Edward loved his family but he was not up to spending the holidays with them – he knew they would badger him with well-intentioned concern about his love life. Ever since he'd broken up with Sasa his family, especially his mother, had been on his case about getting married – though he suspected it was more about making sure he did not get back together with Sasa than about being anxious for grandchildren. He was sure that his mother had arranged for a 'nice, suitable' daughter of one of her friends to join them for Christmas. That was why he had waited until yesterday to tell her he wouldn't be able to join the family in Ghana, so that she wouldn't have time to guilt trip him into changing his mind.

As he made his way to the balcony he admired the tasteful Christmas decorations. In one corner close to the dining area stood a huge silver tree with wrapped boxes, which Edward was certain were empty, lying beneath it. *Trust Lulu to give attention to every detail.* He reached the balcony and immediately his internal radar zoomed in on Sindi. Duma, Lulu's husband and one of his closest friends, welcomed him with a drink. Two associates came over to join them. Edward participated in the conversation half-heartedly. He was more interested in the midnight-blue figure seated on one of the loungers chatting to some of the ladies. At that moment she turned her head and looked at him. Edward's lips twisted into a cocky smile and he raised his glass to her. Her eyes flashed with anger and her mouth set before she returned to her conversation.

Sindi bristled with anger and mortification. She couldn't believe he had caught her stealing a look at him. Then there was that cocky smile he'd given her; it made her hand itch to slap him. *After slapping myself of course. How could I react like that to his kiss? He probably thinks I'm easy prey now.* Out of the corner of her eye she saw him disengage himself from his conversation and head her way. Thankfully one of the other ladies halted him with a flirtatious touch on his arm. Sindi spied as the scantily dressed woman shamelessly flirted with Edward, even though the man she had come to the lunch with could see her. An ever-vigilant Lulu, who had been secretly watching Sindi and Edward spy on each other, jumped up, pulling Sindi up with her.

"Sindi, come, there's one more person I'd like to introduce you to before we sit down to lunch."

Sindi already had a pretty good idea who this *someone* was. She now understood why Lulu had a mischievous grin when she had asked her to get the door. Sindi realised that of the ten guests Lulu had invited only she and Edward were single. Knowing Lulu she guessed this was no coincidence. Lulu was a stickler for planning – any coincidences were planned coincidences. Sindi shot her a warning look but Lulu blocked it with feigned ignorance. Knowing Lulu would stop at nothing to get her way Sindi resigned herself and followed her.

Lulu headed straight for Edward.

"Edward! I'm sorry I didn't get a chance to welcome you when you arrived," Lulu purred while extricating him, with polished finesse, from the flirtatious woman. She gave Edward a hug and a kiss on the cheek. Realising she was being politely thwarted, the woman walked away with a peeved look on her face.

"Thank you for the save, but at my age I know how to disentangle myself from women who are likely to cause complications for me," an amused Edward thanked her.

Lulu laughed. "I'm sure you can but a little help never hurt. I'm so glad you could make it. How did your trip go?"

"Very well … in fact I'll be making a huge announcement soon," he replied.

"That's great! Listen, I want you to meet my best friend Sindi." Lulu practically pushed Sindi at Edward. "She moved to Cape Town from Jo'burg earlier this year. Sindi: this is Edward."

"Actually we've met already, she's the one who let me in." Edward flashed Sindi a secret smile.

"Oh, right! I forgot about that," Lulu said with wide-eyed innocence, not fooling anyone. "Will you two please excuse me? I need to check on the food. I'm sure it's nearly ready." Lulu winked at Sindi and scampered off before either one could respond.

Edward slid closer to Sindi and whispered in her ear, "Seems our hostess has a hidden agenda up her sleeve."

Sindi took a step back. "And either she's really bad at hiding her motives or she doesn't think subtlety is necessary."

"Well, if the kiss we shared is anything to go by, I'd say her instincts are to be commended …"

Not willing to be drawn into discussing any connection between the two of them, Sindi handed him her empty wine glass.

"Excuse me. I'm going to go see if Lulu needs any help."

Edward quickly stepped in front of her, blocking the way, before she could walk off.

"That's the fourth time you're walking away from me. You're starting to hurt my feelings."

"If that's the case then you should learn to toughen up; you're too sensitive. A real man knows how to take punches." Sindi became aware of the curious stares some of the ladies were starting to give them.

"It only happens when I'm around you."

Sindi couldn't help bursting out in laughter. "Seriously? Does that line work for you?"

Edward's lips twitched. "Clearly not."

"Look, people are staring at us. Please let me pass."

"What if I don't want to?" Edward asked.

"You know, you have quite a fan base amongst the ladies," Sindi attempted to change the direction of the conversation.

Edward grinned. "You were discussing me with the other ladies? Did you tell them what an incredible kisser I am?"

Sindi was struck dumb by his arrogance but thankfully she was saved from having to respond by Lulu calling all of them inside. Lulu and Duma took their places at both ends of the dinner table. Sindi found herself seated on Lulu's right. Edward was directly opposite her on Lulu's left. Sindi had a sneaky suspicion Lulu had done it on purpose so as to ensure she could facilitate a conversation between Sindi and Edward. The table was beautifully decorated with gold, silver and splashes of ruby. Lulu served a splendid traditional Christmas feast. The conversation around the table was lively, with lots of wine going around. Sindi enjoyed herself and she even found Edward to be quite charismatic. Afterwards they all moved to the living room to enjoy sundowners until the sun had set and all but Sindi and Edward had left.

"I can't believe you are trying to set me up," Sindi chastised Lulu as they walked back to the living room after Lulu finished giving her a tour of the apartment. Edward was helping Duma tidy up in the kitchen.

"What are you talking about?" she asked with a perplexed look on her face.

Sindi gave her a stern look. "You know exactly what I'm talking about."

"Ok, Ok," Lulu conceded. "I'm sorry. It's just that Edward is such a great guy and you're a great woman. I thought the least I could do was arrange for you two to meet and see what will transpire from that. I promise I had no intention of pushing you onto him."

Sindi glared at Lulu.

"I swear. I wanted things to happen naturally, which is why I didn't tell either of you." Lulu grinned, "Besides you have nothing to complain about. The man is *ab*-solutely gorgeous, he's young and super-wealthy and the best part is that he is the total opposite of that loser you were going to marry – Edward is honest and reliable."

"One, I don't want to talk about Mandla. Two, I doubt our definition of young is the same."

"Thirty-five years old *is* young; *phela* you must remember we aren't 'young and fresh' any more. It's time for us to make way for the younger generation. My friend, don't forget we are 27 years old now."

"I agree Edward is hot but I'm not looking for a relationship right now. I'm not ready. Besides I'm sure Edward is a player – you can't be 'young', hot and rich and not be a player. I *refuse* to feature in anyone's little black book no matter how gorgeous and rich they are. I'm too old for that."

"Edward is not like that. In fact he dated his last girlfriend for eight years before they broke up two years ago. Poor guy, he was so heartbroken."

"Oh?" Sindi's curiosity was stirred.

"Yeah, in fact he hasn't had a serious girlfriend since. Every now and then he has some woman hanging on his arm but I think it's only because he hasn't found anyone worthy yet – not that Sasa was worthy, that's the ex-girlfr—"

Lulu stopped as Duma and Edward entered the living room.

Edward gave Lulu a hug. "Thank you for the wonderful meal; it was delicious. I was telling Duma you two should expect daily visits conveniently around dinner time from now on."

Lulu giggled. "I'll make sure there's enough to accommodate the odd unexpected guest too. It's really thanks to this lady here; she taught me all I know. She's a qualified chef, you know."

"You seem to be forgetting the cooking course you took," Sindi said modestly.

"That was just to refine my skills; otherwise you taught me everything," Lulu replied.

"Well, if today was the student's output I must admit I'm intrigued to experience the master's hand, maybe one of these days I'll receive an invitation to come over and nibble on some of your ... delectables," Edward said. An image of him taking his time and nibbling her private bits popped into Sindi's head. She lowered her head in embarrassment. Edward didn't wait for Sindi to respond. "Lu, thank you once again but unfortunately I must leave now."

"You are most welcome. And thank you for coming," Lulu replied, hugging him again.

Duma turned to Sindi. "Sindi, should I take you home now or do you ladies still want to catch up?"

"No, I think it's time I headed home but don't worry about it, Duma; I'll catch a taxi."

"Do you need a lift?" Edward jumped in. "Where do you stay?"

"Claremont," Sindi replied.

"I'm headed that side. I'll take you home."

"Really? Thanks, man," Duma chipped in before Sindi could respond.

Not wanting to come across as being difficult, Sindi curtailed her protest and simply murmured her thanks.

***

Edward brought his silver Audi RS5 to a smooth stop in front of her building.

"Thank you," Sindi said, unbuckling her seatbelt.

"My pleasure."

"Well, goodnight then."

She opened her door. Edward placed his hand lightly on her knee, halting her. "No nightcap invitation?"

Irritated, Sindi pushed his hand away. "No."

Edward laughed.

"I thought as much. Okay, how about dinner tomorrow then?" He leaned in to her and caressed her cheek with his index finger. "We can work our way to the nightcap ... Or better still how about you make that dinner ..."

"I don't think so." Sindi swatted his finger away and jumped out of the car. Edward caught up to her as she opened the security gate to her building. He held the gate in place, barring her from entering.

"Sindi, I'm sorry. That was a bad joke and I apologise. Please have dinner with me."

Sindi sighed deeply before saying, "I know you were joking but I still don't want to have dinner with you."

"Why not?"

"Goodnight Edward, and thank you for the lift," she said with finality. She indicated that she wanted to go inside. Edward swung the gate wide and allowed her to go in.

"Goodnight Sindi, sleep well," he called out. Sindi simply waved her hand without looking at him.

Edward waited for her to get into the elevator before he went back to his car. He had lost interest in visiting Khanya. He took out his phone and sent her a quick text message, switched his phone off and drove home. Khanya was going to be upset – nothing a spa treatment or a shopping trip wouldn't soothe. A cold shower was in order. Even though Sindi had shot him down several times he couldn't help smiling. The last woman who'd intrigued him as much as Sindi did was Sasa at the beginning of their relationship. He had to see Sindi again.

***

Sindi let herself into her one-bedroom flat. It was cute and cosy, perfect for one person, but after Lulu's apartment, it now seemed cramped and small. Plantation shutter doors separated the bedroom from the living area and the kitchen and living room were open-plan. She went to the kitchen to make herself camomile tea to calm her nerves. While she was drinking the tea she still felt on edge. *Maybe if I soaked in a lavender oil bubble bath I'd feel better.* With that she took her tea to the bathroom. She ran herself a bath and lit scented candles. She soaked in the bath till the water became cold. By the time she got out she was so relaxed she felt like she was floating. She put on her nightclothes and drifted off to sleep easily. A certain handsome somebody dominated her dreams.

Three

The next day Sindi had just finished getting dressed when her intercom buzzed.

"Hello?"

"It's me!" Lulu's voice answered.

"Oh? Come up." Sindi pressed the button to open the security gate.

Sindi was busy fixing her hair in the bathroom when Lulu walked in and stood behind her. Sindi looked at her quizzically in the mirror. "I thought I was supposed to come over?"

"Yes, but I was around the area so I thought I might as well come and pick you up."

"Alright," Sindi said moving to the bedroom to get her bag. "Let's go."

The two women made their way to Lulu's car.

"So are you excited about being asked to organise this party?" Sindi asked as they headed towards the V&A Marina.

"Anxious would be a better description," Lulu answered. "I'm still irked that Mrs Laurant only asked me last week to organise it. I swear she is trying to sabotage me and Duma. She's trying to prove that black people don't belong at the top," she continued, her anger rising, "but it's fine; I'll show her. This will be the best New Year's Eve party Kloofe, Laurant & Moore ever had."

"Yeah, it is dodgy that she gave you short notice. She must have known you'll be hard-pressed finding available suppliers. But it's fine – you have me to help. After all, I'm one of the best event planners and caterers around and luckily I have contacts. Does the firm throw the party every year?"

"We-e-ell, she did acknowledge that it's short notice – she even offered to help me out," Lulu admitted. "The party is for the firm's top clients. It gives the firm a chance to schmooze them. So it's a small party, thankfully. It will be 30 guests made up of the partners, senior associates and the top clients. Normally Mrs Laurant organises it and it's always been at her house and quite a bore really – so predictable and stiff." Lulu rolled her eyes. "That's why I chose a yacht and I'm getting a DJ – none of that Mozart nonsense. Can you believe it? Chamber music on New Year's Eve?"

"If she normally organises the party why did she ask you?"

"She said ..." Lulu cleared her throat before changing her voice to a nasal tone: "'It's only appropriate since they will announcing Doo-mah's appointment as senior associate at the party and what would be better than have his wife organise the annual New Year's Eve party?'"

Sindi cracked up. "That has to be hands down the worst imitation of a white person ever."

"I swear her voice is like that! After all, that woman is old! Yho! I'm sure she has spent the past century smoking. Her voice has this cackling, bleating sound to it."

Lulu mimicked Mrs Laurant again, and Sindi howled with laughter.

"You must be proud of Duma," she said when she was able to speak again.

Lulu broke into a proud grin. "Yeah! Not only is my baby one of two black senior associates at Kloofe, Laurant & Moore, but he's also the youngest. K.L.M is quite a conservative firm, you know, so my baby's done good."

"Do you ever wish you had gone into corporate law like him?"

"On pay day – yes! Or when I see that uber-awesome dress or pair of shoes ... but for the most part I love working for the legal aid clinic and when we are ready to have children it will be easy for me to scale down my work. How about you? How are you finding being an employee instead of an employer?"

"I miss being my own boss but I'm enjoying working at Perfect Event: Paula is a great boss and my colleagues are also wonderful, plus what we do is a lot of fun. I get to plan grand events and parties I wouldn't be able to afford for myself, like this New Year's Eve party I'm working on for this other socialite, Mrs Le Roux. Though I'm not planning on working for someone forever, which is why I'm also catering on the side. I just need to earn enough money to settle my debts and collect a nice amount of savings."

"I have faith in you. I know you'll put your life back together again," Lulu said as she drove into the residents' underground parking of her apartment building. "I thought we could walk down to the marina because it's just here. Then you can have a look at the yacht, and we can decide how we are going to decorate it," Lulu said, parking the car.

"I absolutely love your apartment and the building is gorgeous; it looks like a hotel," Sindi said as they got out.

"It is a hotel; only the top two floors are residential. You should see the penthouses above us. Edward stays in one – *gorgeous*." Lulu sang the last word as she led the way to the marina.

***

Sindi was not a yacht person; in fact she didn't know the difference between a yacht and boat, or if there was even a difference. However, even she was impressed by the vessels moored at the marina. She followed Lulu as she headed towards one of the bigger vessels. They reached a stately craft and climbed on board.

There was a couple waiting for them on the yacht. Sindi gathered they must be crew members since they were wearing what looked like uniforms: white shorts and navy-blue golf shirts with a logo. The man stepped forward to greet them. Lulu accepted his offered hand.

"Mrs Kente I presume?" The man's friendly smile crinkled his deep-blue eyes. His hair was a sun-bleached blonde and his leathery olive skin showed fine lines that were a testament to age and ample time spent with mother nature under the African sun.

"Yes," Lulu replied with a smile. "This is my caterer and party planner, Sindi Mali."

The man shook Sindi's hand.

"I'm pleased to meet you both. I'm the captain, Nick Schultz, and this is our crew director, Kelly Rauls. She is in charge of everything with regards to the needs and comfort of our guests, so if you have any special requests she is the person to speak to."

Kelly stepped forward, smiling. "Pleasure to meet you, Mrs Kente, Ms Mali. Shall I show you around the craft?"

It was clear that Kelly, like Nick, was a sun lover but unlike Nick she still had youth on her side. She had a deeper tan than Nick and her dark hair was caught in a ponytail that was pulled through her cap.

"Thank you," Lulu replied.

A slight breeze made Sindi wish she were wearing shorts like Lulu instead of the sundress and flats she had on.

"*Afia* was built for private comfort and pleasure. She is a real beauty and a joy to sail in." It was clear from Kelly's enthusiasm that she loved the yacht. "She is a reasonably sized craft and personally I think she is one of the best. Some owners can get so caught up in building a grander vessel that the craft loses personality. But this baby has a whole lot of personality." Kelly chatted casually as she started them on the tour.

"*Afia?*" Sindi asked.

Kelly giggled. "Yes, *Afia*. The owner has Ghanaian roots."

"Oh."

"*Afia* has three levels; this is the main deck; where the dining room, bar and lounge are. Then there's the upper deck and lower deck," Kelly said pointing to the respective decks. "She can accommodate up to fifty guests comfortably." She carried on going down the stairs to the lower deck.

"This is the lower deck; this is where the cabins are. Every room is fully furnished to give the comfort of home. There's a fully equipped office behind that door over there," Kelly said pointing to a closed door. "We also have an entertainment room, with the latest equipment." Kelly carried on showing them around. The yacht was the very definition of luxury. The décor was asexual and welcoming. "You and your guests will have access to all the decks but I suspect you'll probably want to have the party mainly on the main or upper deck? We hope that you will have a fantastic time with us."

"How many cabins does she have?" Lulu asked, looking impressed.

"Five double rooms all en suite, and we have guest bathrooms of the highest standard that your guests may use. Let me show you." She moved quickly to a door and opened it. She wasn't kidding when she said it was of the highest standard; the powder room had a modern finish to it. Like the rest of the craft, whoever decorated it managed to get the balance just right: it was neither too feminine nor too masculine.

"I'm happy with everything," Lulu said.

"We were told that you might need waiters; would two be enough for you? Unfortunately it was such short notice that's all I could come up with. Our crew had already been given time off ... But our regular barman has indicated he is available if you need him."

"Really?" Lulu couldn't conceal her excitement. "Oh, thank you, thank you! Yes! I was worried about that and obviously I'll pay them double plus tip. And two waiters will be fine because we'll be serving a cocktail menu."

"Thank you, but that's not necessary. Their wages are covered already and it's my pleasure; after all I'm here to serve your needs."

"You have no idea how much of a help that is." Lulu turned to Sindi. "So now all we have to worry about is the décor; I know you have the menu sorted."

Sindi looked at Kelly. "Will I be able to use the kitchen?"

"The galley? Yes, of course, if you want to," Kelly replied. "Will you require help? Unfortunately our chef won't be available but I can ask his assistant if she will be ..."

"No, that's not necessary I already have an assistant, thank you."

"Shall I show it to you?" Kelly offered, already leading the way.

The galley was as impressive as the rest of the craft. As a cook Sindi felt she was in heaven. The galley was big and spacious. It had modern, clean lines and was equipped with the finest and latest equipment. Sindi knew she would find everything she would need in there. Kelly then took them to the upper deck; which consisted of a Jacuzzi, pool and deck chairs.

The three ladies went back to the main deck.

"*Afia* is available for charter; you can book her for trips anywhere. If you are interested, here are my contact details," Kelly said handing Lulu and Sindi her business card. Nick spotted them and, after wrapping up his conversation with another crew member, he walked up to them, his blue eyes crinkled and friendly.

"Is everything to your satisfaction, ladies?"

"Yes, thank you. We will see you next Friday. We'll come in the morning t–" Lulu was saying when Sindi interjected.

"Actually, Ori and I will come on Thursday to start with the preparations."

"That's fine. We'll see you ladies next week. Just to let you know, we'll be cruising along the Atlantic and will drop anchor at Clifton Beach where we'll have a fireworks display at midnight."

"Great!" Lulu responded with excitement.

"And to confirm: the party is five hours – 8.30pm for 9, and return is 1.30am?"

"Correct. Well, thank you once again. Bye."

Lulu and Sindi shook hands with Nick and Kelly and left.

"Well, now I can rest easily. Everything seems to be under control. Are you sure you don't need them to get you extra help?"

"No, Ori will be enough help," Sindi replied whilst busy planning the menu in her head.

"Do you want to hang out for a while?" Lulu asked her as they neared her apartment.

"No, I should get home. I have to plan your menu and décor though there isn't a lot to do – some fairy lights, extra seating on the main and upper decks … Plus I have work tomorrow – I have that socialite's party I mentioned in the car to plan and set up – so I need all my spare time for yours."

Lulu hugged her. "I wish you would let me pay you. This is not a favour; it's your trade."

"Mmm, I'm not going to have this argument with you again. You are not paying me and that's final. If you want to give back to me then just recommend me to your upper-class friends!"

Lulu grinned. "OK, but *I* will pay Ori, not you."

"Deal."

The days leading up to New Year's Eve went by in a flurry, what with the shortage of time left and Mrs Le Roux's party to work on. Thankfully Lulu wasn't as demanding as Mrs Le Roux. Not that Sindi was worried – she'd had enough experience with difficult clients when she had been running her own company. The difference now was that she didn't have the luxury to tell them to stuff off if they proved to be beyond tolerance.

Soon she couldn't believe it was Thursday, 30 December already. After setting up for Mrs Le Roux's party for the following day, Sindi struggled to leave. Mrs Le Roux had stalled Sindi with her gushing and praises of how impressive Sindi's work was. Sindi found her opportunity to escape when Mrs Le Roux's phone rang.

She was now rushing down to the marina to meet up with her apprentice, Ori, a second year student at the prestigious Cape Peninusula University of Technology's National Diploma in Professional Cookery. Sindi had met her the year before at the annual food trade show, Food Indaba, which had been held at the Cape Town ICC. They had hit it off from the start and had kept in contact. Sindi liked to help students to gain experience as that was how she had started off. So whenever she had a function and needed an assistant Sindi asked Ori to help her out.

Ori was waiting patiently for her at the marina. She was wearing long denim shorts, a white Kingsley School T-shirt and flat pumps. Her braids were piled high on her head in a top bun. A printed scarf made of light material was wrapped around her head in a fashionable bow. She was glad Ori was dressed appropriately. Even though this party was for Lulu, it was important to Sindi that she maintained her professional standards.

"Hello, sweetie," Sindi greeted her with a kiss.

Ori grinned.

"Hello, Sisi." She picked up her bag from the ground.

Even though the age gap between Sindi and Ori wasn't great, Ori insisted on being respectful to Sindi and referring to her as Sisi instead of her first name.

Sindi gave the young girl a smile. "How was your Christmas?"

"Oh, it was wonderful, thank you, Sisi. The whole extended family came down from Bloemfontein to visit us. So it was fun meeting up with relatives I haven't seen in years."

They chatted about Ori's schoolwork and her plans for the future until they reached the yacht.

"Oh, Sisi, this is bea-u-ti-ful!" Ori exclaimed. Sindi shook her head in amusement. Ori had a tendency to stress syllables when she was impressed or excited.

"She is, isn't sh—" Sindi stopped short a few steps away from the boat. Nick was on the main deck with two men. Even though the figure in powder blue and white had his back to her, she knew who it was. As if watching a slow-motion movie reel, Sindi saw him turn his head. A slow, sensual smile spread, his tender lips showing his perfect pearly whites. He looked devastatingly gorgeous: smooth cocoa skin clad in a powder-blue shirt, white knee length shorts and white loafers. The shirt fitted him just right but this time there was no chest preview, and the sleeves were rolled up casually to the elbows. His slim waist was emphasised by the belt that tucked his shirt neatly into the shorts that hugged his strong thighs. Sindi salivated over his solid calves, which had been hidden by his pants the last time. He looked so delectable. She imagined herself spooning him off as if he were ice cream, savouring and playing with his chocolate taste in her mouth ... *mmm* ...

"Sisi, is there something wrong?" Ori's voice brought her sharply back to reality.

Sindi cleared her throat.

"No, hun, I just missed a step, that's all."

She pulled herself together and carried on walking towards the craft. The three men had walked over to the gangway to meet them. Nick offered his hand to Sindi to help her board.

"Ms Mali! It's lovely to see you again."

"You too, Mr Schultz," Sindi replied, returning his friendly smile.

When both ladies were safely on board he gestured to his guests. "Allow me to introduce you to—"

Edward cut Nick off. "No need to, Nick. Ms Mali and I are ... *very* familiar with one another." Edward's eyes travelled her length seductively.

Black or not, Sindi was sure her face was a bright fire engine truck red. Heat burned her face with anger and embarrassment at his innuendo. Sindi's eyes flashed and her mouth set in anger. *How dare he? How dare he insinuate we know each other more intimately than we do? To strangers and in front of my apprentice!* An uncomfortable air settled around them, but thankfully their audience was tactful enough not to react.

The third man smiled at her charmingly. "Well, *I* don't know her. The name is Shawn, Shawn Howard, ma'am," Shawn said with a strong American accent.

"Sindi. And this is Ori, Oratile," Sindi said, her voice shaking with anger. She was grateful to Shawn for breaking the tension. She studied him as she shook hands with him. She had been too distracted mentally devouring Edward to notice how handsome he also was.

"Oh-rah-teal-eeh," Shawn repeated, trying the word out in his mouth. "What does that mean?"

"God's will," Ori responded with a flirty smile.

"That's a beautiful name."

"Thank you," Ori batted her lashes at him. "Where are you from if you don't mind me asking?"

"Chicago, Illinois," Shawn replied proudly.

"Nice." It was clear Ori was awestruck by the handsome man. Sindi was grateful that Ori had a good head on her shoulders so she didn't need to worry about her making a fool of herself and embarrassing her in the process.

Nick turned to Sindi. "Your hired catering supplies and furniture arrived today. We checked everything against the list you e-mailed us and everything is here. We've stored everything in the lower deck."

"Oh, thank you so much. You're such a great help," she said. "Gentlemen, please excuse us; we want to get as much as possible done today."

Sindi headed for the galley in lower deck, making a point of ignoring Edward.

While Ori worked in the galley, chopping and preparing the food, Sindi went looking for Nick or Kelly to help her set up the yacht. She found their office and lifted her hand to knock on the door but, before she could, the door swung open. Sindi and Edward stared at each other. Edward recovered first.

"Sindi! Please come in."

"Uh ... No. Actually I was looking for Nick or Kelly so I'm just going to go look for them."

"Wait, before you go and look for them, may I say something? Please?" he asked.

Sindi wavered. Then she saw Kelly bounding down the stairs. "Excuse me, I have work to do," she replied, turning to Kelly.

Edward watched her talk to Kelly and then the two of them made their way up to the main deck. As he watched them go, he tried to think of how to get back into Sindi's good books. He smiled to himself as an idea formed in his head. He rushed back into the office to make the arrangements.

Four

"Oh. My. Word!" Lulu exclaimed, the next day. Sindi and Lulu had just arrived for the final preparations for the New Year's Eve party later that evening. They stood transfixed at the galley doorway.

"You can say that again," Sindi said.

"Oh. My. Word!"

Sindi and Ori burst out laughing. Sindi rolled her eyes at Lulu as she stepped into the galley.

"What's going on here, Ori?" Lulu asked, "Who brought the flowers?"

Ori dusted her hands off her apron and looked wistfully at the huge and extravagant flower arrangement in the expensive-looking vase sitting on the kitchen island. Sindi was sure the arrangement was made up of at least five big bouquets.

"Hello, Sisi. I have no idea – I've only been here for a short while and they were here already by the time I arrived – but there is a card."

She handed Sindi a small envelope that had Sindi's name written in neat, confident handwriting on the front.

"Thanks," Sindi said, suspicious dread.

With a thudding heart she pulled out the card inside.

Please forgive me, I am truly sorry. Allow me to make it up to you. Have dinner with me tomorrow night at 7.30.
Edward

Sindi's mouth set in a hard line. *What is wrong with this man? Why can't he leave me alone?* Her first instinct was to crumple the card and throw it away but she knew that would only arouse Lulu's curiosity and that she wouldn't rest until she had found out who the flowers were from and what the card said.

Sindi relaxed her face and slipped the card in her jeans' back pocket.

"So? Who sent you the flowers?" Lulu asked.

"It's just a donation for tonight's do," Sindi replied. "Now where should I place them … hmm?"

Lulu blocked Sindi's path. "Nice try. Who 'donated' them? It's quite an extravagant 'donation'. That vase my dear is real silver and it has '*don't even blink my way if you live on a budget*' written all over it and why 'donate' to you and not me?"

Sindi knew Lulu would barrage her with questions until the truth came out, so she gave in, sighing. "OK! They're from Edward."

Lulu grinned. "Edward? Hah …"

"Don't even start," Sindi warned Lulu. "It's just a good wish for tonight."

"If it's so innocent why did you try to hide that Edward sent them?"

"I wasn't hiding it; I just didn't want to say because I knew you'd react this way." Before Lulu could respond Sindi shot her a warning look and nodded in Ori's direction. Even though Ori had gone back to work she could still hear what was being said.

Lulu sent her own look that promised a continuation of their discussion very soon. "Alright, I'm off now. I don't want to be in your hair. If you need anything please let me know."

"Will do," Sindi said, ushering Lulu out.

Sindi and Ori carried on preparing for the party. They finished in good time and even managed to get some rest. As Sindi got dressed in the cabin, her mind wondered to thoughts about Edward. Lulu had told her he was one of Duma's clients so she found herself hoping he would be a guest at the party. There was something about him that both excited and unnerved her. She quickly dismissed the thought, feeling annoyed with herself for even thinking about him.

***

Sindi was at the bow of the yacht enjoying the warm evening air and contemplating the stars when a voice whispered in her ear.

"You look absolutely ravishing. Even the stars pale in comparison to your beauty."

Sindi caught her breath as Edward's warm breath fanned her neck, waking her senses up. *How I wish this man didn't affect me this much – in fact I wish he didn't affect me at all.* Her breathing became shallow and her heart pounded. She felt her nipples tighten against her grey silk dress. The material caressed her naked nipples, creating an erotic pleasure between her legs. Collecting all her strength she kept her gaze steadfast on the sea.

She turned her head to him. "Thanks. You also look quite dashing in your tux," she said, as she returned to looking at the sea.

Sindi had noticed him as soon as he and his date had arrived but she wasn't about to let him know that.

"I think that might be the first compliment you've ever given me. That makes it even more special, thank you." Genuine surprise and delight were clear in his voice.

"What are you doing here anyway? I thought this was a private function for K.L.M.'s most valued clients."

"Well then, I guess they consider me a valued client. Or maybe they were just being polite because they are using my yacht free of charge," Edward answered, laughing.

Sindi's jaw dropped. She whipped her head round to face him. "*This* yacht belongs to you?"

"Well technically, she belongs to my company," he replied as his eyes swept the deck and halted when he spotted the flowers on a coffee table in the middle of the seating area she had created. He frowned. "I don't know if I should be happy or disappointed."

"I'm sorry …?"

"My flowers – *your* flowers. I see you decided to use

them as décor. I'm not sure what that means – either you loved them so much that you decided to display their beauty or you hated them so you decided to pass them on?"

"They're beautiful; thank you for the flowers and your apology," she said finally turning her body to face him. "But I must also admit I did find the arrangement a bit too over the top for my taste."

Edward burst out in laughter. "You're proving to be a very hard woman to please. Is it just me or is playing hard to get your thing?"

Annoyed, Sindi replied, "Oh, please do not flatter yourself. My knowing and valuing my worth has absolutely nothing to do with you." Over his shoulder she saw his date heading their way. "Looks like you've been gone for too long: your date is heading this way and she doesn't look too happy. Excuse me."

He halted her before she could move away. "What about our dinner date? How's tomorrow for you?"

Sindi's anger rose. "You know, asking a woman out on a date while on a date with another woman is low! *Very low.*"

Edward's date reached them.

"Babes, I've been looking for you," she said, putting her arm through his, before looking at Sindi. "Hello," she greeted with a smile even though her body language screamed she was ready for battle.

"Hi," Sindi replied. "Excuse me, Ori is trying to get my attention."

Edward watched her saunter away, wishing he could rewind time and replay the events so that he didn't mess things up with her.

The rest of the evening was a great success. True to her word, Lulu introduced Sindi to potential clients who were impressed with her catering. She even managed to commission three private dinners in the coming weeks. Try as she might, she couldn't stop herself from watching Edward. A few times their eyes met, and once Edward attempted to make his way towards her, but she quickly turned her back to him.

Close to midnight the DJ lowered the music and announced, "Ladies and gentlemen, we have exactly two minutes to say goodbye to this year! So, please, grab a sparkler and get ready for the countdown and fireworks display." Sindi grabbed Lulu and Ori and rushed to the railing so that they could have a good view of the fireworks.

"5, 4, 3, 2, 1 – Happy New Year!"

An extraordinary display of fireworks coloured the dark sky in a multitude of bright colours. Everyone shared the customary hugs and kisses; soon Sindi was faced with Edward. He stared deep in her eyes.

"Happy New Year, Sindi."

He spread his arms, inviting her into a hug. Sindi was unable to resist.

"Happy New Year, Edward," she murmured resting her head on his shoulder.

The hug lasted longer than it should have before Edward's date interrupted them once again.

***

"Happy New Year, Sindi," Farranah greeted Sindi with a smile as Sindi arrived at work the following Monday.

"Same to you, Farranah."

Sindi gave the young receptionist a hug. She braced herself for a blow-by-blow of the latest episode of *The Lives and Scandals of Farranah and Friends*. Every Monday morning Farranah deemed it her duty to update Sindi about her and her friends' outrageous weekend. Sindi liked Farranah but sometimes she wished she wouldn't confide in her so much, especially since she found Farranah and her friends' antics too childish and wild. But, as the only other person of colour besides the tea lady, she supposed Farranah felt kinship with her. She could only imagine how Farranah and her friends had brought the New Year in.

"Paula said I should tell you you must go straight to the boardroom when you arrive. And why aren't you answering your phone? I've been calling and calling. You should see Paula; she's been panicking. Her face is pink with anxiety." Farranah burst out laughing.

"Called me? But my phone hasn't rung?" Confused, Sindi searched her handbag for her phone but couldn't find it. "Looks like I left it at home. Why were you looking for—"

"*Daar is sy*! Where was you? We had been waiting for you forever; you is late." Sonet's thickset body, preceded by her booming voice, came bounding down the passage to the reception area. Sindi checked her watch.

"I'm not late. We start work at 9am and according to my watch it's five to."

Excitement thickened Sonet's already heavy Afrikaans accent. It was so heavy that even when she spoke English she sounded like she was speaking Afrikaans.

"Nee, nee, nee. We have a very important walk-in and we had been waiting for you. Paula wants you to work on dis projekt. Die client arrive here at 8am so he wait for you since." Sonet had lowered her voice to what she considered a soft voice.

"So why not get someone else to work on the project or at the very least take down the brief?" Sindi asked as she was pulled towards the passage leading to the boardroom. Farranah jumped up and followed them.

"He say he wants to wait for you."

Paula came out of the boardroom looking agitated. A look of relief spread over her face when she saw Sindi. Sindi stifled a giggle; Farranah was right: Paula's whole face was bright pink. Paula rushed over to them.

"Oh, Sindi, there you are. Where have you been? Why haven't you answered any of our calls? Never mind, you are here now. Did Sonet and Farranah bring you up to speed? Why don't you go in while I talk to Sonet and Farranah?" Paula said, guiding Sindi into the boardroom.

Sindi walked in and saw a patient-looking Edward sitting alone in the boardroom. Her heart jumped in shock and excitement. Butterflies fluttered in her stomach. She willed her emotions into control.

Edward smiled at her. "Good morning, Sindi."

Sindi pulled herself up to her full height and went to find herself a seat far away from Edward.

"Good morning, Edward," she replied in a prim voice as she sat down.

"I see you are not a morning person. There's no need to be grumpy this early in the morning. You're marring your beauty."

Sindi scowled, irritated by his comment. "I'm not grumpy; I just have a problem with being stalked and fed lame pick-up lines so early in the morning."

Edward laughed. "Are you calling me a stalker?"

Before Sindi could respond Paula walked in with Farranah right behind her.

"Can Farranah offer you more refreshment?" she asked, looking at Edward with a mixture of admiration and eagerness to please.

"No, thank you, I'm good. Sindi?"

Sindi's stomach was agitated, however, she needed something to calm her nerves. "Rooibos for me, thanks, Farranah," she said with a smile.

"Right." Farranah hurried out of the room.

"Well, at least introductions are unnecessary. Mr Boateng—"

"Edward, please."

Paula flushed and fluttered her eyelashes.

"Edward has commissioned us to handle a charity ball he is planning. They'll be launching a children's charity organisation and they've decided to use the opportunity to raise funds as well. Since you two already know each other we felt it would be best if you worked on this event. If it clashes with another project you can hand that project to one of the other account executives." Paula started packing up her notes and file. "Please excuse me. I have another meeting in 30 minutes, so I really have to dash. Mr Boa – sorry, Edward – it was lovely meeting you."

Paula shook Edward's hand and winked at Sindi. Farranah came back with Sindi's tea. As she set the tea down she whispered, "As soon as you are done here you *have* to come to my desk. He's so hot!" Sindi watched with amusement as Farranah threw Edward a flirtatious look before she left the boardroom.

Alone in the boardroom with him, Sindi tried to ease her awkwardness with light chatter.

"So … Your surname is Boateng?"

Edward's lips stretched into his lazy but endearing smile.

"Strange, huh? To think we've shared a passionate kiss yet we didn't even know each other's last names."

"I can't imagine that bothers you very much. I'm sure you are used to it by now. In fact I'm sure you've done more than just kiss a woman whose surname you didn't know."

Edward's eyes narrowed and his face clouded with anger.

"You know, it's one thing to walk around acting and feeling holier than everyone else but it's quite another to judge a person without knowing them. Somehow I doubt even *you* manage to live up to your mighty standards," he said quietly.

Sindi felt ashamed but a fire inside her refused to let her back down and apologise for offending him.

"Seriously? You're going to sit there and act offended? What were you expecting? Was I supposed to be flattered by your ruse? I mean like, really? A charity ball? Come on, we both know there is no such thing. This was just an excuse for you to spend some time with me so that you could spin your charm on me. What is it with you? Why can't you just leave me alone? Do you get off on me being a challenge? Is the thrill in breaking me down? So what was the plan? No, wait, let me guess, I was supposed to be impressed you support a charity and as soon as I fell for your sweet charm the 'ball' was going to get cancelled or better yet – 'postponed indefinitely'?"

Edward's jaw clenched as he sat there listening to Sindi's rant. After she finished her tirade Edward pushed his chair back and grabbed his jacket from the back of the chair.

"It's amazing how such vile bitterness can live under so much beauty." His voice was brimming with anger; gone was the silky baritone she had grown accustomed to.

"For your information there really is a charity function; it was planned and approved just before the Christmas holidays. I thought of you because I was impressed with the catering at the New Year's Eve party and you managed to pull it off at such short notice, not to mention the rave reviews from previous clients of yours who happen to be acquaintances of mine and whose opinion I trust! Not forgetting the fact Lulu has been recommending you to all and sundry, so excuse me for expecting professionalism. Oh, and by the way, I also believe in supporting fellow Africans who are trying to make it, as I know breaking into the business world is especially hard for us!"

Sindi's anger also rose. *Bitter? How dare he call me bitter? Who is **he** to call me bitter? He doesn't even know me!* She jumped out of her chair, stomped up to face him and stood with her hands on her hips.

"Oh really? So what does this 'charity' do?" she asked.

"We raise funds to support children of war, to get them to a place of safety, where we can unite them with family or people willing to take them in."

"If that were true, that would make great P.R. Wouldn't your marketing division be handling it? My instincts tell me you are not a marketing director so it doesn't make sense that you would be here."

"You're right, I'm not. I *own* my company. The reason I didn't involve my marketing department is that this is a personal project and it is close to my heart. I want to be involved in every aspect of this event. I do not appreciate being judged based on non-existent knowledge. I'm beginning to understand why your fiancé ducked out of marrying you. I also wouldn't want to spend the rest of my life with a woman as bitter as you."

A loud crack sounded as Sindi's hand made contact with his face. Both stood there glaring at each other. A chill ran up Sindi's spine as she stared into Edward's cold and menacing eyes. She immediately regretted slapping him.

Edward's voice was calm. "For the record, yes, I'm attracted to you. I've never tried to hide that fact and no matter how much you lie to yourself it's pretty obvious you are just as attracted to me. But, don't worry, I won't be bothering you any more. I'll be taking my business elsewhere." With that he spun around and walked out.

Sindi slumped down into the nearest chair. She knew that somehow she had to win Edward's contract back or else the classifieds might just be her new companion. Even more frightening was the possibility that Edward would never want anything to do with her again. She was sitting with her face in her hands when Farranah walked in.

"And now?" she asked. Sindi twisted her head to face Farranah but, with her head still resting on her hands.

"I messed up, Fay. Big time."

"I guessed, just be grateful Paula was not here to see and don't worry – no-one except me saw him leave. He looked absolutely furious! But still sexy. In fact, sexier.

I love passionate men. That amount of anger can only indicate passion. What happened between you two? Why was he so angry?"

"Farranah, do you mind?" Sindi said, getting up. "Will Paula be out all day?"

"Yes, she has back-to-back meetings, one of which is at one o'clock in Franschhoek."

"Good, please hold all my calls today."

"Sure." Farranah picked up the now-cold tea and patted Sindi's shoulder. "Not to add to your stress, but you need to fix whatever went sour between the two of you asap, because Paula won't be happy if she finds out he walked out angry. She really wants this contract; Mr Boateng will be the first major client in Perfect Event's books. This is the break she's been looking for. She was so happy before she left she promised us all mid-year bonuses and she told everyone they have to give you all the support you require. I mean this is major: Mr Boateng is one of the country's wealthiest and most influential businessmen."

"He is?"

Farranah looked at her with confusion. "I thought you knew him; at least that's what he told Paula."

"No – I do, I just didn't realise how wealthy he is. How do you know?"

"Newspapers, magazines, the internet – paparazzi journalism can be educational, you know," Farranah replied with a wink and grin.

"Excuse me, I need to check my e-mails, there's an important message I'm waiting for."

The first thing Sindi did when she got to her desk was Google Edward Boateng. She typed in Edward Boateng in the search box. The search returned a number of hits including pictures of him. Sindi opened the Wikipedia result.

Sindi skimmed the page:

Edward Boateng hails from one of Ghana's wealthiest families ... first of three children. He has a younger brother who runs the family business in Ghana and a younger sister. ... father was a diplomat and now is an official in the African Union ... millionaire by age 30 ... received an undergraduate degree in business at the University of Cape Town, South Africa and an MBA at Harvard Business School ... returned to Ghana and worked in the family hotel business ... At 25 received the first portion of his trust fund, which he used to open up his first hotel in Cape Town's city centre ... within five years he was running three hotels and had extended his business interests to include property development ... recently bought a charter boat at the auction of the seized assets of alleged Russian mobster Yuri Kournikov ...

The rest of the article carried on about his professional life and achievements. She went back to the search results. She couldn't find anything about his personal life; beyond what she had read on Wikipedia all the other results were business related. She went to his company's website and was surprised to discover he owned the hotel he and Lulu lived in and that his corporation had international business interests. *Well, being a politician's son must have opened many doors for him.* She went to his organisation's contact page. She contemplated calling but knew that without a direct line her chances of getting through to him were non-existent. Besides, she worked in an open office environment and she didn't want any of her colleagues listening in. Making a quick decision, she noted down his business address. She spent the rest of the morning working non-stop, trying to get as much as possible done so that she could leave the office by early afternoon. She had to make sure she got to his office before the end of the day.

Five

The elevator pinged, announcing her arrival at her destination floor. Sindi drew a deep breath as the automatic doors opened out to a large, plush lobby. She braced herself for the tantrum she expected she would have to throw. The walls were panelled with glossy rich wood and the receptionist's desk sat in a nook opposite the elevator. On the walls on either side of the receptionist the name Boateng Group hung in huge gold plating.

Sindi knew that she looked the part in her pleated burgundy high-waisted and narrow-legged turn-ups, cream sleeveless blouse with ruffles running down the middle, and nude heels. Her hair was styled in a neat high-top bun and her Hermès bag was the perfect finish to the outfit. One thing was for sure; they wouldn't toss her out without first giving her the benefit of the doubt. She prayed things would go as smoothly as they had with the building's receptionist on the ground floor. As she stepped out of the elevator the impeccable young receptionist looked up with a wide smile.

"Ms Mali, kindly take a seat. Mr Boateng's PA will be with you shortly." She gestured to the seating area nearby, which was made up of a huge white round coffee table surrounded by white leather chairs and with magazines lying on top of it.

"Thank you," Sindi sat down and picked up a copy of *Forbes* magazine.

"Would you care for something to drink while you wait, Ms Mali?"

"No thanks dear," Sindi answered. If she was to pull off giving the impression she and Edward had an intimate relationship she had to act proud and confident, as if she felt she had every right to be there and be treated well. Sindi leaned back in her chair and started paging through the magazine.

"Ms Mali?" a beautifully made-up, fair-skinned and slender woman dressed in a high-collared sandstone knee-length dress asked. She looked as if she was around Sindi's age.

Annoyed by the woman's contemptuous tone, Sindi cocked her head to one side and answered with a clipped one:"Yes?"

"I'm Thuli Ndlovu, Mr Boateng's right hand." The woman introduced herself without offering her hand. "I've just checked Mr Boateng's diary and there's no record of a meeting with you."

"That's because I never made an appointme—" Sindi started to answer, non-plussed by Thuli's cold manner.

Thuli cut her off. "Well then, in that case I suggest you set up an appointment with Lauren over here. Good day."

Furious at being dismissed, Sindi threw the magazine on the table and stood up, pulling herself to her full height. Growing up she had hated being the only girl as tall as the boys but at moments such as this one she was grateful for her height; she towered over the other woman.

"Hold on, you can't dismiss me like that. I came here to see Edward and I will see Edward."

"I'm afraid Mr Boateng is a busy man; he doesn't have time to see people randomly. Please make an appointment."

"I don't think you heard me; I'm here to see Edward and I *will* see Edward. And, trust me, for *me* he *does* have time."

Thuli's mouth set in a cold line. "I'm Mr Boateng's right hand. I know his diary in and out. I'm afraid he is too busy today; it would be better for you if you made an appointment. If you insist on being difficult I shall have no other option but to ask security to escort you out of here."

"By 'right hand' you mean his secretary, right?" Out of the corner of her eye Sindi saw an amused Lauren duck behind her computer. "Listen, I'm as tired of this circular conversation as you are. Now, if you want to carry on being his secretary, I suggest that you pick up the phone and tell him I'm here." Sindi opened her bag and pretended she was looking for her phone. "Or would you rather I call him myself and get him to come here to put you in your place? I can assure you he won't be very pleased with you; anything that upsets me upsets him more."

The two women stared each other down. For a moment Sindi wondered if she had overplayed her cards. *What if she calls my bluff? After all, gate-keeping is her job. Edward wouldn't be angry with her for protecting him from unwanted visitors.* After what seemed like an eternity, a cold smile spread over Thuli's face.

"Excuse me," she said, walking over to Lauren's desk, appearing confident that she was going to embarrass Sindi. She picked up the phone and dialled an extension.

"Hi, Edward?" Thuli's voice became friendly. "There's a Sindiswa Mali here at reception; she claims you are expecting her."

Thuli's face contored with surprise as she listened to Edward. She moved the mouthpiece closer and turned her back to Sindi.

"Are you sure ... But you have a Skype conference in 15 minutes," Thuli whispered into the phone. "Yes, alright, I'll reschedule." She replaced the receiver and gathered her dignity. With tight lips she said, "He has a few minutes to spare you; please follow me."

Behind Thuli, Sindi saw Lauren silently chuckling gleefully at witnessing Thuli being put in her place.

Sindi's heart pumped hard with excitement. She couldn't believe her victory. Even though she appeared confident throughout her exchange with Thuli, she had been anything but confident. As she followed Thuli down the passage, her hands became clammy as new nervous excitement mounted in her. She worried about the reception she would recieve. Sindi quickly wiped her hands on her pants as they reached a set of double doors.

Thuli opened the doors to reveal a spacious room. On one side there was a desk and on the other a seating area. Thuli headed straight towards another set of double doors and knocked.

"Yes?"

Sindi breathed a sigh of relief. She was glad Edward's voice was back to its warm baritone. That was a good sign – she hoped. Thuli opened the door and Sindi brushed past her. Edward rose from his chair and came around to stand in front of his imposing desk.

"Thank you, Thuli," he dismissed her.

Thuli lingered by the door grasping for a reason to prolong her presence. "May I get you refreshments?"

Edward looked at Sindi. "Sindi?"

"No, thank you. I'm fine," she murmured, her voice caught in her throat. He looked so handsome in his grey pants and silk shirt. Earlier that day, she had been so distracted by her shock at seeing him waiting in the boardroom to truly appreciate how devastatingly gorgeous he looked in grey. The pants were loose, but they still failed to hide his strong thighs, and the silk shirt caressed his torso in a way that made her want to reach out and touch his muscles.

"I'm also fine, thanks, Thuli, and please hold my calls."

"Alright," Thuli answered, frustrated, and closed the door.

Sindi walked back to the door, opened it and then shut it with a definite bang. Edward, who was by now perched on his desk with his arms folded, lifted one quizzical eyebrow.

Sindi shrugged one shoulder and sent him a small smile. "Don't ask …"

Edward stood up and gestured that they should move to the seating area. "I wasn't going to."

Sindi sat on the couch while Edward chose an armchair opposite; a coffee table separated them. "First you insult me, now you come here and bully my staff."

"I was not bullying anyone. I just wanted to make sure we had privacy."

Edward lifted his hands in surrender. "I'm sure you didn't come here for round two, so let's just drop it. Why don't you tell me why you are here?"

Sindi shifted in her seat.

"No, no I didn't," she said wringing her hands. "In actual fact I came to apologise for slapping you. That was uncalled for. I should have never judged you; you are right I don't know you and I have no right to make assumptions based on nothing but my imagination. Besides it's not my place to judge anyone. Lord knows I'm not perfect. It was also narcissistic of me to assume that you'd made up the charity ball, please forgive me."

Edward smiled at her. He got up and went to his desk to pick up a small silver box wrapped with a dark grey silk ribbon. He walked over to her and handed her the box. Surprised, Sindi reached out to accept it. Edward returned to his seat.

"May I open this now?"

"I was hoping you would."

Sindi unwrapped the box with care and curiosity. She lifted the lid. Inside was a miniature plain white flag and on top of it sat a single purple bud. She grinned up at him.

"A purple hyacinth!"

Edward grinned back at her.

"Do you know what the flower symbolises?"

"Yes, it's a 'please forgive me' flower."

"I also was planning on visiting you. I'm sorry for what I said to you and you had every right to slap me. What I said to you was wrong, not to mention cruel, and there's no justification for it." Edward reached over the coffee table to grab her hands. "I'll forgive you if you forgive me?"

Sindi laughed.

"Tit for tat?"

"Yeah," Edward replied shamelessly.

"Let's see, blackmail … white flag … and a purple hyacinth … hmmm … guess I have no choice but to forgive you."

Edward placed a hand over his heart.

"Ouch, old age must be affecting my skills. My charms didn't feature in that list."

"Old age … yeah, that must be it," she replied.

"Hey! I'll have you know I was quite a charmer back in my young days."

They both laughed.

"Ok, I believe you," Sindi replied, raising her hand in surrender before sobering up. "Listen, please don't think that this is the only reason that I came to apologise, but I would really like to organise your charity function ... if you haven't already commissioned someone else, that is."

"I haven't actually. The contract is yours if you want it. I would only be too happy to let you organise it."

"Great! Do you have time for us to discuss it now?"

"Yeah, sure. Let's move over to the conference table over there," Edward said, pointing to a medium-sized oval table standing in one corner of the room. He got up and asked her. "How about some refreshments? Rooibos, right?"

"Yes to both," Sindi smiled. She was pleased he had taken note of her preference earlier.

"Excuse me for a second," Edward said, going to the ante office. The door didn't close properly so Sindi could overhear him and Thuli.

"Thuli, I'd like you to clear the rest of my afternoon and please bring us some refreshments – Rooibos for Sindi and coffee for me."

"But there's a board meeting at 5pm and you told Richard you want to touch base with him before the meeting."

"Cancel both."

"What am I going to say? You know it's hard to coordinate all the board members' schedules!"

"If we can't reschedule another meeting before the next scheduled board meeting it's fine – this wasn't a formal meeting so we don't need the whole board present."

"OK, I'll work something out," Thuli agreed.

When Sindi heard Edward making his way back she quickly ran to his display cabinet, pretending she had been admiring it. He walked over to her.

"Is this your family?" she asked.

"And friends." Edward briefly explained the different people and places in the photos. At the sound of the door opening they both turned. Thuli noted their close proximity as she walked over to the coffee table, where she set down their coffee and tea. They waited for Thuli to leave the room before fetching their cups and taking them to the conference table. Sindi pulled out her notepad from her bag and sat down. They spent the rest of the afternoon brainstorming and planning the charity ball. Before they knew it, it was already past knock off time. Edward looked at his watch: 6pm.

"Unfortunately we have to call it quits for today. I have a dinner date with my parents; if I miss it my mother will be on my case about it, especially since I didn't spend Christmas or New Year's with them. You should have enough to start with."

Sindi checked her watch too. "Gosh! You're right, it's pretty late," she said, packing up.

"May I offer you a ride home?"

"If it won't be too much trouble," Sindi replied.

"None at all," he replied, escorting her out with his hand on the small of her back. They were surprised to find Thuli still at her desk. Edward told her to go home and then he and Sindi left. Thuli stared after them, noting with a sour look where Edward's hand was resting.

***

"How about these?" Lulu pointed to a set of gold and emerald cufflinks.

"Hmm ... I'm not sure. I like them but isn't it a tad intimate to buy him links?" Sindi replied.

It was Saturday. Lulu had asked Sindi to accompany her to shop for a gift to thank Edward for allowing her to use his boat for the New Year's Eve party.

"OK, maybe we should look for something other than jewellery."

"Agreed. Let's go to that new men's shop on Kloof Street – it looks quite interesting."

"Okay, let's go," Lulu said, pushing the jewellery case back to the sales assistant. "Thank you, but we'll go look for something else. If I don't find anything I'll be back for the links."

The two ladies left the jewellery shop and got into Lulu's luxurious Mercedes SL. "So what's been happening with you? It feels like I haven't spoken to you since forever," Lulu asked as she pulled out into the street.

"Nothing much, hey, it's just been work. Oh, by the way, thank you so much – I've been getting calls about catering for private dinners."

"Oh, you're welcome. But really it's all you: people were impressed with the New Year's Eve party. Even Mrs Laurant congratulated me; she went on and on about the food, especially that pastry thingamajig with the cheese and that creamy thing."

Sindi smiled, feeling triumphant.

"That's always a winner. Mrs Laurant was actually one of the people who called me."

"Oh? And how are things at work?"

Sindi rolled her eyes. "I've been the flavour of the week. Edward commissioned us to organise a charity ball he is hosting and all the ladies in the office are absolutely gaga over him, even Paula. That, coupled with the fact that his event will introduce us to an elite potential clientele, has Paula over the moon."

"Really?" Lulu was genuinely surprised. "Now I understand why he's been asking me about you and your work."

"What did you tell him? Was it you who told him about Mandla?"

"No! I would never do that," Lulu answered. "Wait a minute, he *knows* about Mandla? What does he know?"

They had reached their destination and Lulu was parking.

"I don't know how much he knows but he knows I was jilted minutes before I was due at the altar."

"NO!" Lulu shrieked.

"Yes. I'd like to know who's been whispering in his ear and why."

Lulu unbuckled her seatbelt and said, "There's a lounge up this road we can go to and discuss this over a cocktail or two. We'll get the shopping done later."

"Sure," Sindi answered, climbing out of the Mercedes.

***

The waiter set their mojitos in front of them. Lulu took a long sip and closed her eyes in bliss.

"OK, now tell me what happened. How do you know Edward knows about Mandla?" she asked putting her glass down.

Not ready to tell Lulu about her fight with Edward, Sindi glossed over it.

"We were talking and he made a comment about it."

"What was your response?"

Sindi shrugged. "I didn't respond."

"Why?"

"I was too shocked."

"Heeeh … I wonder how he found out? Maybe Duma told him but then Duma would have told …"

"Aargh wethu, it doesn't matter now anyway. Besides, I'm sure I am still the subject of hot gossip; being jilted at the altar and left bankrupt is timeless. You know the worst part about this whole thing is not so much what Mandla did to me but the pity people feel for me. There's nothing more humiliating than pity."

"I'm so sorry you had to go through that, my friend. Duma never liked Mandla. I used to think it was because of their age difference but now I think he probably sensed something we didn't."

"You also never quite took a liking to him."

"Yah, but that's only because I thought someone a little older than you would be more suitable for you. You've always been more mature than our age group and Mandla is a typical Jo'burg party boy and that's not your scene."

"You know what, enough about Mandla – tell me about Edward."

Lulu raised a quizzical eyebrow.

"I'm just curious, that's all. It's unnerving that he knows about me and I know nothing about him," Sindi defended herself.

"I didn't say anything."

"Your expression said it for you."

"What do you want to know?" Lulu asked with a naughty glint in her eyes.

"If you're going to be like this, never mind," Sindi replied.

Lulu laughed. "OK, OK. Let's see … he comes from a wealthy family but he is a millionaire in his own right. He started pretty young, used some of his trust fund—"

"Yeah, yeah, I know all of that. I want to know about *him*, his life, what's he like?"

Lulu gave her another suspicious look.

"Well, he owns the penthouse where we live; actually he owns the hotel. He's a great guy and a hard worker. He is not really into the party life – he prefers a more relaxed lifestyle – but that doesn't mean he doesn't enjoy the mean party or two. He's laid-back and doesn't allow much to ruffle him but boy, you don't want to get on his bad side. Trust me on that one; I've only ever seen him angry twice and that was really scary, even though it wasn't me he was angry at. He's a man in every sense of the word, you know: he is supportive, trustworthy, honest and dependable. In terms of romance … once he commits, he commits fully. In fact, anything he does he does fully."

"Oh? And is he committed to anyone?" Sindi asked as casually as possible.

"As far as I know, not permanently."

"What's that supposed to mean?"

"Well, he was in love with this other woman, Sasa. They were in a relationship for something like eight years and then two years ago she dumped him and moved to L.A. He hasn't dated anyone seriously since then. He does date and all but none of the women he's been out with so far have held his interest for very long."

"Wow, so he must have really been in love with this Sasa."

"I guess, though sometimes I suspected he stayed with her for so long simply because he had no reason to break up with her, more than for emotional reasons. *Yazi*, she tried hard to push them into being an 'it' couple because she wanted her own reality show on VUZU but he refused to play that social game. She decided he was holding her back from her 'true destiny', dumped him and moved to L.A. to become an actress." Lulu took a sip. "You know her actually: Sasa Dlamini, the model and now actress."

Sindi's eyes bulged out of her head, she spewed the sip she had just taken and had a coughing fit. When she regained her composure her voice came out in a surprised shriek.

"*The* Sasa Dlamini?"

"Yep."

"Wow, no wonder he is so cut up. She's gorgeous!"

"Humph ... Like I said I'm not convinced of that."

"How come I haven't met him till now?"

"He was supposed to be the best man at my wedding but remember we had to make last-minute changes because the best man's grandfather passed away and he couldn't attend?"

"Oh yes, now I remember."

"And he had just broken up with Sasa then. That's why she wasn't there."

The waiter came back to check on them and Lulu ordered another round of cocktails.

"So how do you think Paula is going to feel about you and Edward dating?" Lulu asked with a naughty smile after the waiter had left.

"We are not dating and are *never* going to date."

"Lulu thinks thou doth protest too much," Lulu laughed. "Out of curiosity: if you and the superhot Mr Boateng were to date, how would you handle the relationship now that he is a client of yours?"

Sindi shrugged. "I don't know. But it's no-one's business whom I date really. I don't see how it would be relevant as long as we kept our work relationship professional."

"Hmm ... Yeah, you're right I guess. I don't think people mind too much about that kind of thing anyway, but I would suggest you be open and honest with Paula so that she is not blindsided when it comes out. Such things always come out."

"Why are we even having this conversation? I told you – I'm never going to date him. He's not my type," Sindi insisted more to convince herself than to convince Lulu.

The waiter returned with their drinks and they finished their cocktails before finishing the shopping. They went into the store on Kloof Street and looked at a few items before deciding to settle for the cufflinks. They went back to the jewellery store; Lulu paid for the links and had them wrapped.

During the drive home Lulu chatted on about a funny incident that had taken place at her work earlier in the week. Sindi, meanwhile, couldn't forget their conversation about Edward. She wondered if Lulu's assessment of his relationship with Sasa was correct and, if so, why was he still single? Lulu said he had been dating, so why hadn't his heart been captured yet? How often did he date? And how long did these relationships last? Sindi desperately wanted to ask Lulu all these questions but then Lulu would assume she was interested in Edward. *Which I'm not!* So she held her curiosity back.

Six

The following Monday Sindi was working on a proposal when her phone rang. She picked it up without looking at the caller ID.

"Hello?"

"Sindi."

Butterflies fluttered in her stomach. She couldn't help smiling. "Please hold," she requested, jumping up and practically running to the boardroom.

"Edward! How are you?" she said into the phone when she was alone.

"Very well, thank you. Yourself?"

"I'm fantastic."

"Sorry I couldn't get back to you earlier than today. I read your proposal over the weekend and I love your ideas. Tell me how are we going to get the artwork we're going to auction?"

"It's a worthy cause and I know a few well-known and budding artists, or rather I know an art dealer who knows them, plus I'm sure if I drop your name here and there miracles will happen."

Edward laughed. "I think you may be overestimating my powers but, alright, I'll leave everything in your very capable hands."

"Thank you for trusting me with this," she whispered, not ready for the phone call to end.

"Thank you for accepting the assignment," his voice was a sweet caress to her ears and the butterflies in her stomach started to flutter again. He sounded like he wanted to say something but instead said, "Enjoy the rest of your day. Take care. Bye."

"Bye," she replied, disappointed the call was ending so soon.

The rest of the day went by in a whirlwind. Sindi was the last one left in the office and was preparing to go home when her landline rang.

"Yes, Farranah?"

"Thuli from the Boateng Group is on the line for you."

Thuli was the last person Sindi felt like talking to. "I'll take it, thank you, Farranah. You don't have to wait for me, I'll lock up."

"Thanks! Bye."

Sindi heard a click as Farranah transferred the call.

"Hello?" Sindi said.

"Hello. Sindi," Thuli's cool voice travelled over telephone line. "Mr Boateng wants to know if you are available for dinner tonight: 7 for 7.30," she carried on, foregoing all pleasantries.

Sindi's heart thundered.

"Dinner?" she repeated.

"Yes. Dinner," Thuli replied. "He said I should tell you there's someone important he'd like you to meet."

"Oh? Um ... OK, sure. Where?"

"I'll text you the details once I've confirmed the

booking. Do I have to organise a car service for you as well?"

Sindi wasn't sure if it was her imagination but Thuli's voice seemed to be getting colder and colder.

"That won't be necessary, thank you," she answered in the same cool manner. *This woman has a knack of rubbing me up the wrong way.*

"Good." Thuli hung up the phone.

Sindi held the silent receiver to her ear for a while in astonishment. *How rude!* She replaced the receiver and checked her watch. She saw that she had two hours to get ready – *enough time*. She foraged for her mobile phone in her bag and called her regular taxi driver.

***

Sindi looked at herself from all angles in her full-length mirror. Her hands travelled down her curvy figure, which was hugged by a bright-coral knee-length dress. She had bought the dress because she had fallen completely and utterly in love with the colour and the length-long industrial zipper at the back of the dress. Satisfied with the reflection, she sat down on the bed. Facing the mirror, she picked up her curling iron and styled her hair into side-swept curls. Just as she was putting the finishing touches to her hair her phone alerted her to a message. It was the taxi driver, waiting outside. Sindi took one last look in the mirror and smiled at herself. She picked up her bold print clutch bag, slipped her feet into her cobalt-blue heels, then raced to the waiting taxi.

As the taxi came to a halt in front of the hotel, a doorman came to assist Sindi out of the car.

"Have you come to dine, ma'am?" he asked as he escorted her into the hotel.

"Yes."

"The restaurant is that way." The doorman pointed to a softly lit hallway to the right side of the entrance.

"Thank you," she replied with a smile and headed towards the restaurant. The hallway had contemporary and luxurious décor. It led to a cool, chic and elegant lounge and bar and had exquisite crystal chandeliers hanging from the ceiling that created an ambience of luxury and glamour. She spotted Edward almost immediately. He was standing at the bar next to an extremely tall and slightly older-looking man. They were talking to a woman who was sitting on a bar-stool. As if he could sense her, Edward turned to look at her. She felt a now-familiar warmth spread through her as his eyes travelled the length of her body. The man and the woman followed Edward's gaze. His intense stare made her acutely aware of her sexuality; she felt like a goddess. Unconsciously her neck extended and her breasts pushed out as she pulled herself upright. Edward glided over to her, their eyes never breaking contact.

"You look absolutely sensational," he whispered in her ear.

Sindi closed her eyes as she inhaled his intoxicating spiciness.

"Thank you, you look quite handsome in your dinner

suit, but I'm sure you knew that already," she teased.

"Complimenting me is becoming quite a habit for you."

"Don't get too used to it."

A sexy laugh rumbled out of Edward's chest.

He offered her his arm and together they covered the distance to their dinner companions. At the bar, he led her to the stool they had been keeping for her.

"Sindi, this is one of my closest friends, Hermann Awola and his wife Grace. Hermann, Grace, this is Sindi Mali," Edward introduced.

Hermann kissed Sindi's hand while his wife inclined her head in greeting. Both their faces were lit up with friendly smiles. Sindi looked at Hermann and his wife with interest; she had never seen anyone who looked like them before. They had perfectly round faces and heads, their complexions were so dark they looked almost blue, and both had the Sindi had ever seen. Hermann and his wife weren't particularly good-looking, but it was impossible not to bathe in their warmth.

"Pleasure to meet you, Miss," Hermann said. Each word was enunciated with such care and delicacy it was as if he was trying out the word for the first time.

Sindi tried to place his accent but failed; it was soft and the words sounded round.

"I apologise to say this about your woman, my friend, but she is even more beautiful than I imagined," Hermann said looking at Edward. The two men grinned at each other above her head.

"She is beautiful, but unfortunately she is not my woman, my friend." The unspoken word "yet" hung in the air.

A confused look crossed Hermann's face. He looked at each of them before taking Sindi's hand and bowing over it.

"I sincerely apologise for my presumptions, Miss."

"That's alright," Sindi said with a warm smile. "And please call me Sindi."

The maître d' cleared his throat discreetly to attract their attention. "Excuse me sirs, madams, your table is ready. Please follow me."

The two men were charming throughout the meal. Their narrations of their varsity days had Sindi and Grace in stitches. They also told Sindi about the adventures they'd been through after varsity – some of which were recounted by Grace.

"…This man worked three jobs so that he could put himself through university and he still managed to be top of the class. You cannot help admiring such dedication and tenacity," Edward said proudly as their coffee arrived.

Sindi looked at Hermann with admiration. "Wow, that really is something. That must have been hard. You are quite inspirational."

"He is, isn't he? He's also one of the reasons I have such a solid work ethic and he was the inspiration behind this charity we've started."

"He's my inspiration too," Grace added, smiling at her husband.

Like Hermann she also spoke in a soft voice but hers had a distinctive English lilt. Hermann's hand covered Grace's and his thumb stroked her knuckles.

"Oh really? Why?" Sindi asked, picking up her coffee and smiling at the happy couple.

A shadow crossed Hermann's face. "I'm one of what is known as 'the lost boys of Sudan'. Do you know about them?"

Embarrassed about her ignorance, Sindi admitted, "Not really; wasn't there a movie or book about it?"

"Yes, there's even a stage play. My people, the black people of Sudan, who live mostly in South Sudan, spent decades being attacked by the Islamic government and militia supported by them. We lost our homes, our families and children were orphaned. The war began in 1956 but 1983 was the catalyst – that year the Islamic government attempted to impose the sharia law on everyone and one day out of the blue they just attacked. Many of us young boys escaped because we were grazing cattle at cattle camps, which were some distance from the villages." Hermann laughed humourlessly. "To think a chore I hated so saved my life. I remember that day vividly. I still have nightmares about it."

Sindi noticed Grace squeezing her husband's hand.

"When I was 12 my parents had taken my sister and me to visit our grandparents in a village near our city. That morning, my grandfather had asked me to go check on the livestock. While I was doing that I heard really loud noises, so I went outside the camp to check and all I could see was smoke. I ran and hid in between tall reeds and waited for the noise to stop. Then I ran to the house. There, as I walked through the burning house, I found dead bodies and fatally wounded people, including those of my parents. In the kitchen I found my grandmother lying on the floor in a pool of her own blood. She kept repeating my sister's name and pointing to a cabinet."

Hermann choked at the memory.

"I opened the cabinet and found my little sister frightened and crying silently. I grabbed her and ran outside to hide in the big tree behind the house. A few minutes later the house collapsed. I didn't know what to do or where to go. For a week we slept in the back yard under the tree, eating its fruit and hiding in its branches during the day. Finally, some people came and took us to a displacement camp in Sudan. I knew I had to be strong for my sister. I had to take care of her. I was her only family now. Later I learned that they were taking boys strong enough and turning them into soldiers, and the females were being raped and sold to slavery. So, after two weeks at the camp, I woke my sister up one night and I ran away with her. We ran into other children like us and we began our long journey to safety. Other children joined us along the way. During the journey I witnessed the most horrific things, things I wish no other child to experience."

Hermann's voice broke. Edward patted his friend's shoulder and added, "Our charity will raise money to fund aid groups all over the world. We want to help children, not just from war-torn countries, but children who are victims of child labour, pornography, human trafficking, slavery, abuse etc."

"I am completely speechless," Sindi said, in awe of how someone who had endured so much could still be filled with so much warmth and friendliness. "Where's your sister now?"

"Back in South Sudan. She is a doctor," Hermann said with a proud smile. "She, like my wife and me, is determined to help rebuild our country. We had hoped that the peace we had enjoyed just recently would last. This new threat of war is quite disheartening, but one must keep faith alive. We will continue with our efforts as we cannot allow war or the threat of it to destroy our country completely. Hopefully one day soon we shall find lasting peace."

"Mmm," Sindi agreed. She turned to look at Grace. "Did you also go through the same experience, Grace?"

"No, I was fortunate. My father's company had sponsored him to study for his doctorate at Oxford University so our family was living in England at the time. But obviously I was affected indirectly – South Sudan is my home country and I too lost family members."

The rest of the conversation went back to lighter topics. Soon it was time to leave.

"It is such a shame to cut the evening so short; however, we have an early-morning flight out tomorrow," Hermann apologised.

"Don't worry about it, I understand," Sindi replied.

Edward called for the bill and settled it. Hermann and Grace escorted them outside. Edward handed the valet his ticket and the valet brought Edward's car.

"Goodbye, brother. I will see you in Chicago," Hermann said hugging Edward while Grace hugged Sindi. Hermann then turned to hug Sindi.

"Miss Sindi, it was lovely meeting you. Bye."

"Yes, it was. Can I please have lunch with you when we come back? Just you and me; the men can find other things to amuse themselves with," Grace added with a warm smile.

"I'd love to; please let me know when," Sindi replied.

Hermann and Grace went back into their hotel as Edward guided Sindi to his waiting car, his hand resting on the small of her back.

He opened her door and waited for her to settle in comfortably before moving around to his side. Edward started the car and soothing neo-soul sound wafted through the car. Sindi, feeling contented after the wonderful evening, sank back into her seat with a smile on her face.

"Bilal?" Sindi asked Edward as the car pulled off.

He looked at her in surprise. "Yeah. You know his music? I thought only hip-hop and neo-soul fans knew him."

"Nah, I think he's popular with people who generally like conscious and soulful music."

"He's what I consider good music: deep, soulful and meaningful."

"Mmm ..." Sindi agreed.

They fell into a comfortable silence, both being transported by the music into their own thoughts.

"Thank you," she said softly after a while of driving in silence.

Edward shot a quick glance at her. "For what?"

"Dinner, an evening out, good company and ..." she lowered her voice, feeling shy, "showing me your heart. It's nice to see there's more to you than obnoxious arrogance."

Edward laughed.

"I couldn't help noticing that Hermann looks slightly older than you?"

"He is. He's like my older brother. Because of what he went through in his childhood he was behind in his schooling. That's how we ended up schooling together."

"Makes sense," Sindi said leaning back.

The rest of the ride to her flat was pleasant; the conversation flowed easily, even playful at times.

Sindi felt somewhat sad when Edward pulled up outside her building. She unbuckled her seatbelt and looked at him.

Smiling shyly and lowering her eyelashes she asked, "Would you like to come in for a nightcap?"

Edward laughed as he undid his seatbelt. "I knew if I bought you dinner I'd get a nightcap. But I'm afraid I have to decline. I have an early flight out of the country tomorrow and I have a few things to wrap up before my trip." He leaned in to to her and dropped his voice a notch to a sexier note. "But I promise to take you out when I get back ... then we can have our nightcap and you *must* wear that dress – that zip is driving me extremely wild."

He dropped his head to meet her face but stopped short of her lips, waiting for her to give him the green light. Her heart pounded against her ribcage. He was so close to her she could taste his breath. She tilted her face to his. With a smile he closed the gap between them and captured her lips in a fiery, passionate kiss. His hands moved under her hair to support her head. His fingers kneaded her scalp, causing her to tilt her head back in pleasure. He took advantage of the free access to her neck, kissing and nibbling his way down her throat. Heat crept between her thighs. She grabbed his shoulders. Her lips searched for his mouth, capturing his lips and devouring them. Fired up by her excited response, his right hand trailed her body while the left hand carried on massaging her head. It slowly moved over her neck and shoulder, down her breast, across her stomach, to her hip and past her thigh, leaving a trail of tingles. When his hand reached the hem of the dress she tried to open her legs but the dress restrained her. She shifted to pull the dress up but he halted her and broke the kiss.

He rested his forehead against hers as they both tried to control their heavy breathing.

"Wh-what's wrong?" she asked, when she was finally able to speak.

Edward kissed her. "Nothing, baby. You are so beautiful and sexy and you feel so warm," he caressed her face. "And that dress ... that zip ... but this is just not the right place to do this," he smiled wryly. "Unless you want to give your neighbours a show."

Sindi lowered her lashes and once again embarrassment washed over her.

What is it about this man that brings out the hedonist in me?

He kissed her again, then moved away from her. "Come. I'll walk you to your door."

He jumped out of the car and went around to open her door for her. He walked her up to the security gate. He lifted her chin and dropped a slow kiss on her lips, then lifted his head.

"Hold on," he whispered.

Edward ran back to the car and came back holding a CD. "I want you to listen to the track 'Something To Hold On To.' Let me know your think when I get back."

Sindi took the CD and read the cover: Bilal, *Love for Sale*.

"Think about what? The song?"

"Listen to the song. You'll understand." He leaned in to her and kissed her cheek. "I want you to know I mean every single word in the song." Edward took her keys from her hand and opened the security gate.

Sindi nodded and gave him a small smile. "Have a safe trip," she said before she went inside.

Edward waited until she got into the elevator before returning to his car and driving home.

***

Sindi let herself inside her apartment. She set her handbag on the kitchen counter and headed straight for her DVD player and slotted the CD in. She skipped to the track Edward told her to listen to and sat in front of the player. The first instrumentals of the song entered and then Bilal's humble voice began crooning. Sindi bobbed her head along to the catchy hip-hop influenced beat and concentrated on the words. She smiled as she listened to Bilal confess his feelings to his intended, telling her how she had captured him and how he would love to get close to her. When the song ended she replayed it.

Seven

Sindi looked at her watch in anticipation. Edward was due back from Chicago this afternoon. He had extended his trip by an extra two weeks. The past three weeks had been amazing. They'd been in daily contact, e-mailing and Skyping each other. This was her new night-time ritual: every night before falling asleep she closed her eyes and recalled their last encounter. She was falling for him and even though she knew she was on dangerous territory she was beyond resisting him any longer. He always managed to surprise her. One afternoon during one of their e-mail chats she had told him she was craving a Hudson's burger. Half an hour later she'd received a delivery from Hudson's. She smiled as she remembered that day. All the ladies at the office thought it was very sweet of him, but then again they'd all fallen for his charms the first day he had visited the office.

Sindi discreetly extricated herself from her client, who was busy asking questions of the venue manager. She listened to Bilal's song every day. She couldn't wait for Edward to return so that she could tell him he no longer had to wonder what he had to do to win her, because he had already, and that, yes, she was also attracted to him and wanted to be with him. His track record warned her that any romance with him would be short-lived but she just couldn't stop herself from falling for him. She took out her mobile phone to send him an e-mail, but her phone lit up. She grinned when she saw the caller ID.

"Hello?" she answered, without waiting for it to ring.

Edward's hearty chuckle greeted her back. "You're that excited, huh? Couldn't you at least let it ring the customary three times first?"

"Why should I hold myself back from something I want to do?"

Edward chuckled again. "Why indeed? Listen, babes, I know I said we'll have dinner when I come back, but dinner time is too far away. Any chance you are available for lunch?"

Sindi smiled. "You're back already? Give me about two hours. I'm currently viewing venues with a client. After that I'm all yours. I'll take the afternoon off; no-one will know."

"Mmm ... I like the sound of that. Do you want me to pick you up?"

"No, I think it'll be better if I catch a taxi. Where do you want to meet?"

"Somewhere by the beach – Clifton or Camps Bay. Text me when you are done and we'll decide then."

"Alright."

Edward's voice dropped a notch. "Can't wait to see you ..."

Sindi smiled dreamily as she held the receiver against her ear. She saw her client and the venue manager head towards her.

"Bye, Edward, my client is coming back," she responded, hanging up.

***

"You sure look happy," Sindi commented as Edward helped her into her seat. He had arrived at the restaurant before her. He looked every bit the young, successful millionaire in his shorts, casual shirt and loafers.

"Of course I'm happy. I've been missing you like crazy. These past three weeks have been a lifetime and now you are finally here in front of me."

Sindi blushed. "Hah ... and your business trip has *nothing* to do with your good mood?"

"Well there's that too, but right now I'm over the moon because of you."

The waiter arrived to take their order.

"So what is it about your trip that has made you so happy?" Sindi asked after they had placed their orders and the waiter had gone.

"We've finally officially sealed our multimillion-dollar deal. Which is why I'm asking you to cater the small cocktail celebration I'll be throwing next Friday. It will be a few business associates and their partners, around twenty or so people – you will be paid of course."

"Ah-ha! The real reason for this impromptu lunch date. Buttering me up, Mr Boateng?"

Edward threw his hands up.

"OK, I admit it," he answered playing along. "You busted me. Did it work?"

"Mmm ... Not quite, I need some more softening up."

"I've always loved challenges. Be prepared for the best soft-soaping you'll ever receive."

Sindi burst out laughing. "Are you sure you are up for it, gramps?"

"Gramps?"

"Yeah, gramps. Your game is so old school it really gives you away."

Edward chuckled. "How is my game old school?"

"Where do I start? Let's see ... well, there're the cheesy lines—"

"What? What cheesy lines?"

Sindi couldn't help the laughter that bubbled out of her.

"Don't you listen to yourself when you speak?" 'That's the fourth time you are walking away from me. You're starting to hurt my feelings.'"

Edward also laughed. "How's telling the truth cheesy? You *were* hurting my feelings."

"Then there's the Bilal CD you gave me. That was short of you making me a mix tape. In fact, I'm sure if you'd had the time you would have made me a mix tape."

"But what's wrong with that? Every time I heard that song I thought of you and I found it very apt for how I feel about you," Edward confessed, smiling.

Sindi blushed and lowered her eyes for a moment, before looking up at him again.

"There's nothing wrong. It's just that having a song for someone is kinda ... corny and old school."

Edward picked up a small package with a bow taped to it that was sitting on the chair next to him and waved it at her.

"I guess I shouldn't give you this then," he said, teasing her.

"Is that what I think it is?" Sindi asked, laughing.

"Yes, and you're no longer getting it," Edward replied returning the package to the seat, laughing along with her.

"OK, OK. I take it all back." Sindi was having a hard time controlling her laughter. "Please give it to me. I promise to appreciate it and *all* the time and effort you put into making that mix tape."

Edward shook his head at her. She battered her lashes at him.

"I promise I won't make fun of you."

Edward shook his head again.

"I promise to cater your cocktail party," she tried again, holding her right hand up while her left hand lay over her heart.

"Deal!" He relented, laughing. Edward handed her the CD.

Sindi flipped it over and read the typed track list. With a fresh burst of laughter she read the list out loud.

"Jodeci … Keith Martin … Jagged Edge … Shai … After 7!"

"You promised not to laugh!"

"I'm not laughing. I'm just … it's just … I mean … gosh, when was the last time I heard these songs or *any* song from these artists! This takes me back, thank you," she said, still laughing hard.

"You seem to know these artists so that means either I'm not as ancient as you make me or you're as ancient as I am," Edward replied, partly offended.

"No, it means I have an older sister who used to blast these songs when she was home during her university holidays. By the way, I was still in junior primary at the time."

"And I was still in high school, not varsity," Edward countered with mock indignation.

"Probably grade 12."

"Maybe I'm chasing after the wrong sister here … what's your sister's number?"

"Sorry, my sister is happily married to a tall, dark and handsome man and they have two kids."

Edward sat up straight and grinned.

"Then I'm her type. I'm also tall, dark and handsome."

"Tall? Yes. Dark? Yes. Handsome? Arguable," Sindi retorted, enjoying the friendly banter.

"I'm black. All black men are dark and handsome."

"Really now?" Sindi was beside herself with laughter.

The waiter arrived with their food. While they were eating, they chatted about their families and careers. Afterwards, Edward convinced her to take a tour of Cape Town on the red open-topped bus with him. As the bus weaved through the streets of Cape Town, Sindi basked in the joy she felt at spending time with Edward. After the tour they went out for dinner at a restaurant in

Gardens. Sindi was sad when the evening came to end. She dreaded saying goodnight to Edward as they pulled up in front of her block of flats. When Edward asked to see her the following evening she couldn't hold back her smile as she agreed.

***

"Thank you for another charming evening," Sindi said with a coy smile as Edward brought his car to a halt in front of her building. She and Edward had been out every day for the past week.

Edward grinned back at her. "'Another'? Does that mean grandpa still has some life in him?"

Sindi laughed. "Yeah, seems there's something still to be said for old school after all."

Edward leaned over, and kissed her. Sindi responded immediately, wrapping her arms around his neck and pulling him closer. Edward ran his tongue across her lips, causing her to let out a low moan. Her tongue reached out for his and she pushed her breasts against him. Their tongues danced together, then Edward's tongue trailed the roof of her mouth and she shuddered. Slowly Edward lifted his head and rested his forehead on hers.

"You still haven't given me your response," he said, in between heavy breaths.

"To what?" she asked, just as out of breath as him.

Panting, Edward answered, "Before I left for America I gave you a song to listen to."

Sindi laughed and gave him a peck on the lips. She whispered, climbing on top of him, "Do you really need to ask? I would have thought this – here, right now – would have been enough of an answer."

Edward showed his delight by accepting her kisses. This time Sindi broke off the kiss.

"Should we go in for that overdue nightcap?"

Edward dropped a small kiss on her lips.

"I'm sorry baby, but I'm pretty bushed. These past few days have been hectic. I've had to work past midnight – you know with the deal I told you about – because my partners are in different time zones our meetings have been at awkward hours. Next time. I promise."

"That's the second time you're rejecting me. You're starting to hurt my feelings," she mimicked.

Edward laughed.

"Eish, the youth of today! No manners whatsoever. Come, let me walk you to your door."

Sindi climbed off him and adjusted her clothes while Edward opened her door for her. He walked her to the security gate. As he was about to close the gate after her she stopped him.

"This is not my door. My door is upstairs."

Edward growled good-naturedly. "You're turning out to be a demanding queen."

"You're the one who offered to walk me to my door. I didn't ask you to."

They got into the elevator and ascended to her

third-floor flat. Outside her door she attempted to cajole him.

"Are you sure you don't want to come in?"

Edward grabbed her around the waist and pulled her in to him. "Baby, I would really love to – I'm sure you can also feel how rock-solid I am. But I'm so tired I'll pass out on top of you."

"When I said nightcap, I really meant nightcap. Besides if you are that tired how are going to manage to drive—" She stopped mid-sentence as an unwelcome thought crossed her mind. *Just because he's spent the past week with me does not mean I'm the only woman in his life.* Shutters came down over her face and her eyes lost their sparkle as an impenetrable cloud gathered over them.

"Oh," she said, quickly turning around to her door and attempting to open it with a shaky hand.

"Sindi—"

"It's alright, I understand, drive safely. Bye." Sindi slipped through the door but before she could shut it behind her Edward blocked it with his foot.

"Sindi, it's not what you think," he said following her in after she gave up trying to shut him out.

"At the beginning of last year I was humiliated and made a fool of – that is an experience I'm *not* about to repeat, not knowingly anyway."

"There's no-one else, I promise you. I'm going straight home, I am honestly tired," he said.

Sindi stared at him for a long time before deciding to give him the benefit of doubt.

"OK, I believe you," she relented but still visibly upset.

Edward took both of her hands into his. "Baby, I promise I'm telling you the truth."

"What happened to the woman you took to Lulu's New Year's Eve party?"

"Khanya? Khanya and I weren't serious and our relationship is over."

"How long were you two together?"

"About five months, but like I said it was a casual relationship."

"And me? Would I be another Khanya? Would I also have an expiry date looming above me?"

"That's unfair and you know it."

"Is it?"

"She knew that a long-term relationship between us was not going to happen and she was fine with that, which is why she didn't make a fuss when I ended things with her."

Sindi crossed her arms and stared at him sceptically. "Really? She was very territorial that night. When did you break up with her?"

"OK, I may have just stopped communicating with her without saying something to her."

Sindi threw her hands up in disbelief and walked into her bedroom. Edward followed her. "I promise I haven't spoken to her or seen her since that night. In fact, all I did was drop her off and she got mad because I refused to go inside or take her home with me." Edward grabbed Sindi's hands in desperation. "Baby, please believe me.

Ever since I met you on Christmas Day I haven't been interested in any other woman. In fact, that night I was supposed to see Khanya but after dropping you off I went straight home."

"You don't get it, do you? Leaving things hanging means that you are leaving room to go back to her anytime."

"Even if I wanted to she'd never take me back. Khanya is not the type of woman who hangs around waiting for a man to come back. She understands cut communication means it's over. I will prove to you no-one is expecting me; I will sleep over. Here, take my phone. You will see no-one will attempt to call or text me."

Sindi searched his eyes and all she could see was sincerity and honesty.

"Alright, I believe you," she whispered. "And you can keep your phone."

Edward hugged her tightly. "Thank you. I know how difficult trusting me is for you."

Sindi extricated herself from him. "Well, you said you are tired, so let's just go to sleep."

She walked to her closet and selected from her lingerie basket a pink and purple lace chemise that she knew would go well with the pink lace panties she was wearing. *Just because nothing is going to happen, doesn't mean I must pull a Bridget Jones on him.* She went to her en-suite bathroom to change. After changing she washed her face, brushed her teeth and applied a little mascara – just enough to enhance her eyes but still be unnoticeable. *No harm in waking up looking pretty.* By the time she came out, all the lights were off except for the lamp on her side of the bed. Edward's muscular back was facing her. She stood in the doorway bathed by the bathroom light watching the slow rise and fall of his back. She fantasised about running her hands over his sinewy back muscles, over to his pectorals then across his torso down his pelvis bone. Edward turned over and smiled sleepily at her, interrupting her fantasy. He patted the empty space beside him and reached his arm out. Smiling, Sindi turned off the bathroom light and climbed into his waiting arms. She switched off the lamp. The moonlight shone through the half-slit blinds, enveloping the room in semi-darkness.

"You are so beautiful. I want you so much right now it's taking all my strength to resist you but I want the first time we make love to be proper. I want to give you all the attention and care you deserve. I promise you baby, your body will be loved so thoroughly you will be unable to get out of bed," he breathed into the back of her neck sleepily.

Sindi shivered at the promise; she instinctively knew his promise was not an idle one. She settled into his strong body, her behind pressing against his solid testament to desire, and drifted off to an erotic sleep.

Eight

Sindi woke up in the middle of the night burning with heat to find herself half-straddling Edward's thigh. Edward's hands were inside her underwear kneading her behind.

"Oh, baby, what are you doing to me?" he whispered fervently, holding her tightly. He flipped her under him, settling himself between her legs, which accommodated him voluntarily. "I can no longer control myself. When I woke up to you grinding my thigh …"

Edward's lips descended upon hers, nibbling and teasing her until she felt like screaming in frustration. Sindi lifted her legs and wrapped them around his waist. She tilted her pelvis to him. Edward could feel the heat emanating between her legs but decided to ignore her hint. Instead he grazed his teeth along her jawline. Sindi tried to hint again by lifting her pelvis, but this time she slid up and down against his manhood. Once again he ignored her and pushed down her strap to reveal a breast. He captured the nipple between his teeth. Sindi gasped in pleasure. Unable to withstand the torment any longer, she locked her ankles around his thighs and attempted to swing Edward underneath her but he was too strong for her.

"Please, Edward, please," she whimpered.

"Patience, baby." He massaged the other breast with his tongue.

"No! Now!" she roared.

Edward stared down at her in the semi-darkness and saw the pleading look on her face. He lifted himself off her to remove his briefs, and then he reached for a condom in his pants' pocket. He had hardly finished rolling the condom on when she pushed her underwear aside, lifted her pelvis, grabbed him and pushed him down into her with passionate force.

"Oh!" They both called out in unison.

For a moment neither one moved. They both lay motionless, savouring the moment and acclimatising themselves to each other. Slowly and gently Edward retracted his manhood a bit and adjusted himself for her comfort. Bending down he kissed her tenderly.

"You're so eager you're going to hurt yourself. You nearly took all of me in," he said, chuckling with wonder and amusement. With great care he began to move slowly inside her. Sindi soon found his rhythm and joined in. Once again she attempted to push him underneath her, and this time Edward didn't fight her. Sindi took him with her as she climbed into heights of ecstasy in a dance as old as time. Soon she felt an overwhelming swell surge from within her. Her body began to tense. Edward switched positions with her. Tightly she gripped his wrists, which were balancing his weight on either side of her. Her legs slid down his waist to lock with his ankles. Recognising the signs, Edward urged. "Not now, hold it, baby."

"I caa-nnn't!" Sindi cried, unable to control the wave

hitting her. Almost immediately she felt a second wave build up.

"Together, baby, together." Edward's voice was hoarse and constricted by passion. He lifted her arms above her head and their fingers linked as they both came in unison. Edward's head whipped back, and a deep growl stemmed from the pit of his stomach. The length of his body stretched out tautly while her body collapsed into the bed with a shuddering cry. Sindi lay on her back, sensitised and trembling, and he collapsed on top of her. They both lay completely satiated and spent, with him still inside her and their arms wrapped around each other. Neither one wanted to move. When Edward started to soften, he slowly pulled out of her, removed the condom and went to throw it away. He returned to bed, pulling Sindi onto his chest.

"*That* was beyond words," Sindi said sleepily.

"I second that."

He kissed her slowly before drifting off to sleep.

***

The first rays of sunlight woke her up. Sindi smiled at the memory of their lovemaking. She stretched her body languidly before climbing out of bed to make coffee and toast. She'd just finished brewing coffee for him when Edward walked into the kitchen with a towel wrapped around his waist. Sindi admired his physique. He reminded her of an ancient African warrior.

"Coffee and toast?" she asked with a smile.

Edward grabbed her and kissed her thoroughly.

"May I have you instead?"

Sindi laughed, pulling out of his embrace.

"Don't start or else we'll be late for work."

"So?"

"So I'm an employee, not an employer like you," she said, plopping a teabag into her cup.

She set two plates, a coffee mug and the coffee pot for him, as well as the toast rack on the small round breakfast table in the middle of the kitchen.

"Jam and butter?" she asked, opening the fridge.

"Just butter please," Edward answered, sitting down.

"I also like butter on my toast."

Edward buttered a slice of toast.

"I love your place. It's cute."

"Meaning it's small," Sindi said.

"No, my English is not failing me – meaning cute."

Sindi laughed.

"Do you know what the true meaning of cute is? Ugly but lovable."

Edward joined in the laughter.

"You said it, not me. All I meant was it's pretty and inviting. It's like you. There's a balance to it – like for example your flat is feminine without being too girlie."

"Thank you."

"As for the breakfast … I thought you're supposed to be a great chef."

"This is all your performance deserves."

"What! I happen to think I was quite the stud!"

"Exactly. *You* think, *I* don't think."

"Damn, your standards are pretty high then. Alright, you want my real stuff? I'll give you my real stuff but beware, I come with a disclaimer: 'At your own risk'."

Sindi's eyes glazed with passion as she thought about their lovemaking. She couldn't imagine anything greater than what she had experienced just a few hours ago.

"I'd better shower and get dressed before other more desirable activities overtake my morning," she said, standing up.

"Shall I pick you up from work today, so that we can buy everything you will need for the cocktail party tomorrow?"

"Thanks, that would be a big help," she replied, walking out of the kitchen.

***

Edward's car was already parked outside when Sindi left her office. She hurriedly got into the car before any of her colleagues came out and saw her.

"Hi, baby." Edward leaned in to kiss her before reaching to the back to retrieve a bouquet of pink and purple tulips. "I hope these are more to your liking."

"They're beautiful! Thank you!" Sindi squealed with delight, hugging him with one arm.

"Glad I got it right this time," he laughed, pulling out

of the parking lot. "So, where do you want to buy your ingredients?"

Sindi pulled out the shopping list she had compiled during her lunch break.

"The V&A Waterfront makes sense, doesn't it?"

"The V&A it is then," he said, making his way towards the Waterfront.

After they finished shopping Edward insisted on taking her out for dinner. They went to a restaurant at the water's edge. Wanting to take advantage of the scenery and the warm summer evening they chose a table outside.

***

Sindi checked her watch. It was nearly eight o'clock at night.

"I think it's time we made our way home," she suggested.

Edward signalled to the waiter to bring their bill.

"Do you still want to come over to see what crockery I have?"

"Yes, I need to check if I'll need to bring some of mine and I'd like to pre-prepare what I can as I won't have much time tomorrow. That's why I prefer weekend gigs – at least then I have lots of time to cook."

The waiter returned with the bill and the card machine. Edward paid the bill and pulled a couple of bills from his wallet to tip the waiter. Judging by the look on the waiter's face, Sindi guessed his tip had been more than generous. Edward stood up and waited for her to pass him before he followed her out of the restaurant, his hand resting on the small of her back.

In his hotel's underground private parking garage, Edward pulled up in his parking space. They got out of the car and headed towards the private elevator. Sindi spotted both Lulu and Duma's cars. She silently prayed they wouldn't bump into them. She was not ready to share the recent developments with Lulu as she wasn't completely sure what they meant.

Edward entered a code on the keypad and his own private elevator doors opened. He escorted her inside and pressed the button to the penthouse. When they reached the top floor the elevator pinged and the doors opened onto a carpeted entrance foyer bathed in warm lighting. In the middle of the foyer stood a fairly large round table made of polished walnut wood. On it sat an impressive array of deep-blue and purple flowers peppered with softer shades. Sindi looked at the flowers and then lifted a teasing brow at Edward.

He shrugged.

"Probably my housekeeper."

The panelled walls as well as the set of double doors ahead of the elevator were made with the same wood as the table. The doors had gold handles and on either side of the doors were oversized wingback chairs covered in taupe canvas. Above each chair hung a painting. To the left of the elevator was a wide door made from the same wood.

"That's the helpers' quarters," Edward explained, following her glance.

He headed straight for the double doors and opened them. They entered the penthouse. Like Lulu's apartment it was open-plan, except his had a panoramic view and was double storey. To the immediate left was a staircase. The left side of the apartment had a huge terrace that faced Robben Island. On the right was another terrace facing Table Mountain.

"Would you like me to show you around?" Edward asked politely.

"I'd love that, thanks," she replied.

In the open-plan section were the bar, sitting room and dining room. A polished walnut-clad wall separated the dining area and the TV room, which was set up with the latest entertainment equipment. The modern state-of-the art kitchen led off to the terrace facing Robben Island and into the TV room.

"Upstairs are all the bedrooms," Edward said. He pointed to a set of two closed doors. "That's the study and the guest toilet, and then there's a gazebo, pool and Jacuzzi on the rooftop."

"Your place is beautiful," Sindi complimented, taking in all the luxurious furnishings and décor. The polished wood and sturdy leather furniture created a distinctively masculine atmosphere but the mix of cream, brown and taupe around the room, as well as the blend of leather and fabric and the strategic floral arrangements, added a touch of femininity.

"Thank you," Edward replied, heading for the intercom phone hanging in the kitchen. He picked up the receiver and pressed a button. "Francis? Can you please come to the penthouse? Thank you."

Edward turned to her.

"Would you like anything?"

"Anything?"

"Anything."

"In that case …" Sindi sauntered to him and wound her arms around his neck. "How about working on those skills we discussed this morning?"

"Mmm … Beautiful. Sexy. Smart. And psychic as well?" Edward punctuated each word with a kiss as he pushed her up against the marble kitchen island. They explored each other's mouths. Sindi caught his lower lip between her teeth and sucked it. Edward groaned, lifted her off the island and pushed her against the fridge. They continued kissing. One of his hands pinned both her arms above her head while the other leisurely unbuttoned her sheer shirt.

He had just undone the last button when a discreet male cough interrupted them. Sindi peered over his shoulder and saw a youngish coloured man in a black suit and an elderly black woman in a blue-grey housekeeper's uniform standing in the doorway. Mortified that an elderly woman had just witnessed her licentious behaviour, she hid her face in Edward's chest. Edward placed one hand on either side of her to shield her with his body while she tidied herself up.

"Please wait for us in the lounge; we'll be with you in a moment," he said over his shoulder.

When Sindi was decent he chuckled and dropped a quick kiss on her lips.

"You OK, babe?"

Still mortified, Sindi was unable to let out any sound so she just nodded.

"Good," Edward said pulling her along.

She wrenched her wrist out of his grip.

"No way!" she whispered.

"You have to be introduced to them sometime, might as well be now. Besides, it'd be rude not to."

Knowing he was right she followed him out of the kitchen. The man and woman were sitting in the lounge. The man jumped up when he saw them.

"Sindi, this is Mam'Sheila, our housekeeper, and this is Francis, our butler. Mam'Sheila, Francis, this is my girlfriend, Sindiswa Mali, but you may call her Sindi."

Edward dropped a kiss on Sindi's forehead.

"Hi," Sindi waved shyly by Edward's side. Her head was reeling from the realisation that he'd given her the official status of being his girlfriend.

"Hello, my child," Mam'Sheila greeted with a warm smile.

"Hello, mama," Sindi replied politely.

Francis just grinned at her. Sindi had a pretty good idea why he was grinning. Edward took out his car keys from his pocket and handed them to Francis.

"Francis, I have packages in the boot. Please arrange for them to be brought up, thank you."

"Yes, sir," Francis bowed before exiting. Sindi nearly laughed at his formality.

"Excuse me," Sindi picked up her handbag from the couch where she had dropped it and headed for the guest toilet. In the toilet she sat on the seat to compose herself. When she felt better she got up and carefully touched up her make-up, and then returned to the lounge. Edward was sitting in the TV room alone watching Al Jazeera. Sindi snuggled against him. Edward's arm snaked around her.

"How crazy was that?" she giggled.

"I felt like a teen caught doing things he has no business doing."

They both laughed.

"Has Mam'Sheila left?" Sindi asked looking around.

"Yes, she just wanted to know if there's anything I needed as she was turning in," he answered.

The front door opened. Francis and two hotel workers walked in carrying the groceries.

"Just put everything on the counter. I'll sort it out myself. Thank you and goodnight," Edward said following the three men so that he could lock the front door after them and set the alarm.

He returned to Sindi with a wicked grin on his face. "Remind me what we were doing before?"

Sindi dived out of his oncoming embrace giggling.

"Sorry, that ship has sailed. I have work to do. We can't leave the food out here, especially the perishable stuff. Plus I need to make the filo pastry and it's a lengthy process."

Edward sighed. "I suppose I should help you. The sooner you finish, the sooner I can have my lecherous way with you. I still don't understand why you didn't just buy the frozen pastry."

"I told you I like preparing my own pastry. I abhor that frozen stuff."

They worked together harmoniously. Edward proved to be quite adept in the kitchen. By the time they were done it was nightfall. Sindi collapsed on the TV room couch in exhaustion. Edward brought her a glass of red wine, which she took gratefully. He took off her shoes and massaged her feet. Soon the massage turned erotic. A deep sigh escaped from Sindi as she sank further into the soft cushions. Edward looked at her relaxed face. She looked so beautiful and serene lying there with her eyes closed – his loins stirred. His gaze dropped to her feet. He found her deep-red toenails extremely arousing. He took one big toe into his mouth and sucked it before turning his attention to her sole, paying extra attention to her instep. This was her first time experiencing a foot seduction and she was surprised to find that she quite enjoyed it. Edward's mouth moved to her other foot and repeated the seduction as his hands travelled up the length of her legs and undid her pants. Slowly and sensually he slid them down her legs, his clipped fingernails scraping her legs in the process.

Sindi moaned.

"You enjoying yourself, baby?"

"Mmm-mmm," she croaked.

"Good, this is only the beginning."

He dropped her pants on the floor. His mouth moved to her ankle. His teeth nipped it, causing her to stretch out her leg. Edward chuckled. His mouth slowly travelled up her leg, nibbling its way up, only pausing to explore the back of her knee. Sindi's body tingled. Edward's mouth travelled further up. She felt warmth build up between her legs as his mouth worked on her inner thigh. Sindi reached down and pressed his face against her most feminine part. She rubbed herself against his nose. Edward could smell her inner heat. The smell gave him a head rush. His manhood strained inside his pants but he was determined to pleasure her fully first.

Sindi moaned with desire again.

Edward gently turned her around onto her stomach. He drew in the sight of her backside, clad in boy-leg cut lace, staring up at him. His big hands covered her buttocks and kneaded them erotically.

"I love these panties; they're sooo …" he whispered, his voice hoarse with passion. With a grunt he tenderly bit her bottom.

Sindi let out a small yelp. Her breasts filled and became heavy, they cried out for freedom. She reached behind her to unhook her bra but Edward halted her.

"No, baby, I want to love you properly tonight. There'll be no rushing."

"You said I wouldn't want to get out of bed if you do and I need to be at work tomorrow."

Edward chuckled. "Don't worry, you'll have plenty of time to rest ... I'll be gentle with you."

He kissed her mouth before resuming his work on her buttocks; he licked, nipped, spanked, played with and kneaded them. His mouth trailed across her bottom to her other leg. He repeated the exercise he had performed on the other leg but this time heading towards her foot. His fingers hooked her panties and followed his mouth. Soon she was free of her panties. Sindi turned around and opened her legs, inviting him in between. Edward accepted the position, kicking off his shoes. Sindi sat up. Her eyes were cloudy with passion, never breaking contact with his. She unhooked his belt and pants and slid them off him. Next she followed with his shirt, then her blouse.

They sat on the couch, him kneeling between her warm thighs in only his briefs and her sitting up with only her black lace bra on. She ran her hands across his ridged chest before peppering it with soft kisses. Her attention then moved to his tight nipples. She licked and nipped them, enjoying his sounds of pleasure. She lifted her head and accepted his mouth in a hot kiss as her hand moved down to play with his manhood. It felt big and as hard as steel. She broke the kiss and looked down, noting the bulk protruding through his briefs. She couldn't believe the size of it. Edward saw where she was looking and smiled proudly before descending on her mouth, pushing her back into the couch. Sindi returned his kiss with equal ferocity. Edward's mouth travelled to the side of her chin, licking down her neck to the curve of her collarbone and shoulder. Sindi's eyes flew open as she discovered with shock a new erogenous zone. Her legs wrapped tightly around his waist and her womanhood rested on his bulge. She writhed against him. He could feel her wetness through the fabric of his briefs. She pulled him tightly against her pleasurably sore breasts with one arm while the other pushed his face into the base of her neck. Edward rocked along with her. Soon he felt her body tense and her breath quickening. He picked up the pace while he carried on kissing her neck. Sindi cried out and bucked as liquid heat slid inside her. Edward felt her body relax, and moved his lips back to her mouth. He kissed her slowly until he felt her pulse and breathing slow down. He broke the kiss.

"Look at me," he whispered.

Sindi opened her eyes and gazed at him through slit eyes. Holding her gaze, Edward moved his hand over her tender breasts and stomach to between her thighs. He slid his index and middle fingers inside her and rested his palm against her clitoris.

He smiled at her. "You're on fire."

Sindi closed her eyes and groaned as his fingers worked

inside her and his palm rubbed her clit. His mouth sucked a deliciously sore nipple through the flimsy lace brassiere. The rough material grazed the sensitised nipple, causing her to squirm and making his long fingers reach deep inside her.

"That feels good!" she whispered.

"I'm not close to being done with you, baby," Edward promised.

Edward's free hand slowly pushed down one bra strap. Her sensitive body tingled as the strap went down, and then he pushed her bra cup aside. Edward watched as her hardened nipple sprang up. He reached around her and with her help removed the bra altogether. He watched the other nipple rise as well. Sindi gyrated on the hand inside her. Edward dipped his head and teased her breasts. Sindi grabbed the hand inside her and rode it hard. She felt a third finger slide in and the pace of his hand pick up. A second wave fiercer than the first one built up; she could feel her womanhood pulsing with heat and she squeezed her legs tightly together.

"Open your eyes, baby. I want to look into your eyes as you come."

Sindi struggled to open her eyes and only managed to crack them open. Finally she let out a scream of pleasure as the crescendo hit her.

By the time she was done she was half-hanging off the couch with her head on the floor. She lay with her eyes closed and her body feeling slightly numb.

"Come on, baby, we are nearly done," Edward whispered.

"No, I can't," she said.

"Yes, you can. I promise I won't work you hard."

"No, you don't understand. It's too much."

"Come on, baby," Edward kissed her nose. "You can do it."

He flicked his tongue over her clitoris. Her body twitched in response. His lips played with her clit. In a swift move his briefs were gone and his hot pulsing shaft was rubbing against her, awakening her body. Sindi opened her eyes. Edward teased her opening with the tip of his hot shaft. Sindi moaned and ran her hands across his torso.

"Wait a sec," Edward said, climbing off her.

He opened the drawer of the huge coffee table next to them. He felt around till he found what he was looking for. He put the condom in his mouth and closed the drawer. Sindi in the meantime had climbed off the couch and had gone on all fours. She smiled naughtily at Edward over her shoulder and beckoned him with her head. Excited, Edward quickly slipped the condom on and positioned himself behind her. One of his arms snaked around her waist while his other hand played with her breasts. Sindi moaned lifting her spine, causing her buttocks to press against his manhood. She arched her back and wiggled her butt. Edward slowly swayed his manhood back and forth, rubbing against her. Sindi moaned moving along with him. Edward felt her heat beckoning him in. He slipped a fingertip inside her and felt hot liquid. Unable to endure the torture any longer, Sindi reached between her legs and guided him inside her.

A deep sigh escaped from within her. She tried to sit up but he gently pushed her back down on the carpet and pulled her hips up. Slowly he moved inside her, holding her hips in place. She joined in. They moved together, building another wave. He felt her buck and shudder beneath him as he rode her from behind. A climax built up inside him and he rode her faster and faster till the hot wave hit him and he collapsed on top of her, arching her to him, but he carried on riding her as he could feel another oncoming wave, this one more intense. At the same time her body was also preparing for another wave. His hands covered hers on the floor and their fingers entwined. A spurt of strength bubbled inside her. She pushed herself off the floor onto him so that she was sitting on his lap. She took over the ride from him and soon had them both crying out in unison. Then she wrapped his arms around her and they both collapsed onto their sides, her body twitching with sensitivity.

"Did you say I wouldn't *want* to get out of bed or I wouldn't be *able* to get out of bed?" she asked a few moments later, smiling.

"I can't remember. It may have been both. Why? How do you feel?"

"Both. I don't want to get up and I can't – even if I wanted to."

Edward chuckled, "I'm a man of my word."

"Yes, you are," Sindi yawned. "You know what I just realised? None of the windows were covered and we had the lights on the whole time. Someone with a good pair of eyes or binoculars could have been watching the whole thing."

"And wishing they were either you or me," Edward added kissing her shoulder.

He eased himself out of her and took off the condom. Then he rested his hand on her hip and they both fell into a deep sleep.

***

Sindi woke up as she was being swept up in Edward's arms. "What's going on?" she asked sleepily.

Edward kissed her nose.

"Nothing, babe, I'm just putting you to bed. We can't sleep on the floor the whole night," he said as he carried her to the master bedroom. Sindi relaxed herself in his arms. Edward entered the expansive room with a bed so huge it had to be custom-made. Edward pulled the covers back and placed her in the middle of the bed. Sindi watched from behind half-closed lids as he moved around the room. The blinds and curtains hadn't been closed, so the moonlight shone brightly and she could see his strong cocoa body clearly. She felt a stirring between her legs.

"Where are you going?" she asked.

Edward turned at the sound of alarm in her voice.

"Downstairs to fetch our clothes and your bag."

"Oh."

When Edward returned he climbed behind her and held her tightly in his arms, but it still took Sindi a while to relax. Edward walking out of the bedroom after just putting her into his bed had alarmed her. It reminded her of his preference for casual relationships. She couldn't stop thinking about Lulu's words: *After his break-up with Sasa no woman has been able to capture his heart*. She closed her eyes and attempted to fall asleep but her mind wouldn't rest and questions kept buzzing in her head: How long would her relationship with Edward last? Was her decision to be with him a smart one? Would the short-lived happiness be worth the inevitable heartbreak?

Nine

"Good morning!" A voice shouted.

Sindi grunted and turned over only to have the sunlight hit her eyes. She turned back again.

"The time is 5.55am. The temperature outside is 15 degrees Celsius," the voice continued.

Sindi kicked Edward.

"Why is there a woman in your room? Can't she see we are sleeping?" she asked in isiXhosa.

"First, ouch. Second, that woman is the alarm."

"My, aren't we fancy?"

The six o'clock news on the radio began to play.

Edward groaned. "I guess we have to get up."

Sindi pulled the covers over her. Edward nudged her playfully.

"Woman, get up. You owe me breakfast."

"Oh please, I don't *owe* you anything. Besides, it takes me all of two minutes to whip up scrambled eggs and toast."

"What? Scrambled eggs and toast? Woman, after last night's performance you owe me a five-star breakfast."

"Last night's performance? That was only a notch up, hence the breakfast will only be a notch up."

"A notch up? Let me remind you of last night," he said climbing on top of her. He pinned her arms above her head and gunned straight for the spot on her neck.

Sindi squealed. They rolled around in the bed until she cried out, "OK, OK. I remember, I remember."

"You're lucky I have a breakfast meeting at 7.30, otherwise I'd be all over you."

Sindi looked at the time on the alarm clock next to his side of the bed: 6.07.

"What? So you're leaving now-now?"

"Not now, after I shower and dress," he answered getting out of bed.

"Yeah, what I mean is: we can't even have a quick breakfast together?"

Edward leaned over the bed and kissed her.

"Sorry, baby."

Sindi felt a lump in her throat. She didn't know how to translate what was going on. *Why didn't he tell me about this breakfast meeting yesterday? Am I supposed to only feature in one part of his life? But he did introduce you to his staff as his girlfriend. Yes, but men always say things they don't mean. You could just be another Khanya. For all you know he may have lost interest in you already.*

Edward stood next to the bed watching her emotions play across her face. His loins stirred. She looked so sexy. All he wanted to do was reach out and hold her tight. He watched her retreat behind her eyes, giving him that impassive look of hers.

"OK," she finally said.

"Baby, what's wrong?"

"Wrong? Nothing. Do you mind closing the curtains? I'd like to get out of bed."

Unashamed, Edward walked naked to the window and pulled the blinds down. He turned the slats so that enough light entered the room whilst giving her privacy.

Feeling the need to create some sort of distance between them, Sindi slid out of bed and shielded herself from him by covering her breasts with one arm while her other hand covered her most private part. She looked around the room for her clothes.

"You have a gorgeous body. You should be proud of it, not hiding it," Edward said quietly.

She ignored him.

"More especially from me," he continued.

When she didn't answer he continued. "I've seen all you have to offer and I like it. Remember the lights were on the whole time last night. And I carried you to bed – there's nothing to hide from me."

"What makes you think I care what you think about my body?"

Sindi found her clothes. She went to the bathroom and closed the door. Edward followed and wondered what to do, standing outside the door. He could hear her trying to lock the door. He pushed open the door and let himself in.

"The door doesn't lock. What's going on? Five minutes ago we were laughing and playing, then I tell you I have a breakfast meeting, and now you are back to building walls and obstacles?"

"I told you: nothing is wrong."

"Bullshit! Obviously something is wrong. You're

trying to lock me out of rooms in my own house as if I make you feel threatened and uncomfortable!" Edward shouted.

Sindi looked up at him with a range of emotions running through her. She felt frustrated, angry and stupid for falling for him. She still wanted him but she was scared of how she would be affected when it all ended. The lost look on her face pulled his heartstrings and made him change his approach. He blew out of his mouth in frustration and lowered his voice.

"Do you want me to cancel my breakfast meeting? Should I take the day off so we can hang out?"

"No!"

"Then what? Baby, please talk to me," he pleaded.

Sindi sat on the side of the bathtub, her eyes watering.

"It's just that … I don't think I can do this."

Edward sat next to her.

"Do what?"

"This – you and me. I don't think I'm meant to date anyone. I was with the same guy for three years and it turns out the relationship I thought we had only existed in my mind. And before that all the relationships I was in were just as disastrous." Sindi broke down crying.

"I trusted Mandla, he was going to be my husband, and I lived with this man for two years. Two years! Only to learn I never really knew him, he was a complete stranger to me. Do you know how scary that is? I was going to marry someone I didn't know; a liar, a criminal and a cheat."

Edward hugged her, listening.

"I don't know how to trust. I want to trust you. I want to believe you. But I'm finding it difficult. You don't threaten me; you *scare* me with these feelings I have for you. I want you like I've never wanted another man before. Physically you take me to heights I've never been to and the joy I feel when I'm around you is indescribable. Mandla entered my life like a whirlwind, making everything bright and exciting, then left me in cinders. I'm just scared the same thing will happen again. You were with someone when we met, then you just left her. I know you said you two had an understanding but I can't help wondering how soon it will be before you trade me in too."

Edward kissed the top of her head and rubbed her back, encouraging her to cry into his chest.

"Oh, babe, please don't ever say that again. You're not an inanimate object that can be traded in. You are far more special than that. And don't you ever compare yourself to Khanya ever again. Honey, Khanya is a lovely woman. She's beautiful and fun. I won't lie: I enjoyed her company but she had nothing long-term to offer me. I didn't get as far as I am in business without being able to read people. One thing you need to understand is that women like Khanya are motivated by greed for material things – that's their main priority in a relationship. She knows how to attract a man and keep him happy but she lacks …" Edward started stroking her face. "… your warmth and your values. You are beautiful, capable and independent. You carry yourself with pride. She is a hardened woman with only physical gratification to offer. All she is interested in are the ring, the bank account and power; if those aren't all on offer, she's happy with the gifts. You aren't like that." Edward smiled at her and gave her a peck. "Some man out there might see something long-term in her but that man is not me," he continued before taking her mouth in his.

Sindi responded immediately, dropping her clothes to the floor and throwing her arms around him. Edward lifted her astride him. She went willingly. Edward's mouth went to her neck. Sindi extended her neck, giving him greater access. Edward found her spot. A deep sigh escaped her. Her nipples tightened and heat gathered between her legs. Sindi's back arched and she rocked back and forth on top of him. She felt his shaft grow underneath her, heightening her own arousal. Edward grabbed her buttocks and kneaded them as he sucked her nipples. Sindi's fingernails lightly roamed his back, causing him to flex his back muscles. Sindi lifted his face. She ran her tongue across his lips, coaxing him to part them and when he did she captured his sweet tongue and sucked it. Edward let out a groan. He lifted Sindi and set her down. He got up to retrieve a condom from the bathroom cabinet and slipped it on. He sat on the floor and leaned his back against the wall. He bent his knees so that his pelvis could tilt to an angle that would allow her to accommodate him comfortably.

Sindi bit her lower lip and lowered herself onto him.

She giggled, "Now I can see us in the shower door."

Edward laughed and pushed her back so that her back rested on his bent knees.

"I want to watch your breasts bounce," he said as he ran a hand over them. Slowly Sindi began moving up and down him, growing more passionate as her climax approached. From his position Edward had a good view of her breasts bouncing up and down, mimicking her movement. Recognising she was near climax Edward lifted her off him and moved her in front of the bathroom basin. He turned her around so that she was facing the mirror.

"Look at your eyes," Edward whispered in her ear.

Sindi looked. The passion in her clouded eyes surprised her. She couldn't believe that the sensual, sexy woman staring back at her was her.

"Now I want you to watch yourself as you come," Edward said as he entered her from behind. Sindi swallowed hard as she felt him enter, her eyes fluttered closed. She pulled his head to hers over her shoulder and kissed him hard.

"No, open your eyes," Edward whispered to her again when they broke their kiss.

She opened her eyes.

"Look at yourself."

Again, she obeyed. Edward pumped into her faster. Sindi gasped and felt around the marble basin for something to grab on. Her body tensed as the wave drew closer. She looked at her eyes: her irises had changed to a very deep brown and her eyes looked cloudy. She combusted as liquid heat slid inside her. Her body went limp. Edward's grip around her waist prevented her from collapsing to the floor.

"Hold on baby, I'm about to come too."

Edward let out a deep growl as he came. He guided them both to the floor. The cool tiles felt good against Sindi's hot skin. They lay on the floor for a while regaining their energy.

"Do you want to tell me about your ex?" Edward asked cautiously.

Sindi was quiet for a while.

"I started catering in my second year in culinary school, after my sister asked me to cater for a baby shower she was hosting for her friend. I started getting jobs after that. I built capital and after graduating I set up my own catering company. I was quite successful and needed to expand in order to meet demand. I approached a business consultation firm to help me with a business plan and to advise me. That's where I met Mandla. He assisted me and we soon started dating. Six months later he suggested I expand my services to include event planning, which made sense. He quit his job and joined me as a partner. I remember being flattered that he had so much faith in me he was willing to resign from his job. He was really good at finding clients and networking and my strength is in planning, organising and implementation. We worked so well together we were really successful. A year into the relationship we got engaged and moved in together. And the rest I guess you know; all along he was embezzling funds and running around with other women behind my back."

"I'm really sorry you had to go through that." Edward kissed her back and squeezed her. "Come, we need to shower. I'm late already," he said standing up.

Sindi took his offered hand and also stood up. She stepped into the huge shower.

"Aren't you going to join me?" she asked.

"No, I'll use one of the other en suites. I can't be close to you without wanting to touch you and your naked body is going to prevent us from leaving this room."

Disappointed, Sindi pouted.

"Alright, but you'll be missing out."

Edward kissed her and left her to her toilette.

Sindi took a quick shower. She took the fluffy grey towel on the rail and wrapped it around her body. She went to the bedroom to grab her make-up bag. A quick rummage produced hand cream. She shrugged and decided to use it for her face, elbows, knees and shins. She tried to think how she could work her clothes so that it wouldn't be obvious she hadn't slept at home but her previous day's outfit was not a flexible one. She had no option but to go home first. *At least my meeting is not until 10am.*

Edward walked into the bedroom. "Remember the day we met I mentioned to you I have a sister?"

"Yes."

"Well, she stays with me but she has just recently graduated from UCT and is taking a year off before continuing her studies. So she has gone to stay with my parents in Ghana. I had a quick look in her room, and there are some toiletries and clothes there. I know you ladies are particular about your toiletries but maybe you'll find something useful there. And she is around your height so I'm sure you'll find something to wear."

"Thank you. Which room is it?" Sindi asked heading for the door.

"The second to the last room down the hallway."

Edward's sister may have been the same height as Sindi but she was definitely skinnier. Sindi finally decided on a short-sleeved dress. Luckily for her it seemed Edward's sister had done some shopping before leaving, as Sindi also found a toothbrush still in its packaging and brand-new underwear still with tags on. Sindi had just finished getting dressed when Edward walked in.

"Wow, you look beautiful."

"Really? In this old thing?"

They both laughed. Edward kissed her.

"Babes, I'm sorry but I have to rush so I won't be able to drop you off."

"That's alright, I'll catch a taxi."

"I actually have another suggestion. You've got a driver's licence, don't you?"

"Yes."

Edward handed her a set of keys. "Take my sister's car. You'll find it in the parking garage: a red BMW with the licence plate TNX DD. I asked Mam'Sheila to arrange the purchase of toiletries for you; please give her a list of whatever you need."

"Thanks, but it's not necessary," she smiled at him.

"It's no trouble, I'll also arrange for a change of underwear and clothes."

"Underwear? No, that's too personal. It's Friday anyway. I can bring some of my stuff over the weekend."

"Don't worry, I wasn't going to ask Mam'Sheila. I was going to ask Thuli."

"Mmm ... still, I'm not comfortable with that."

"OK then. Bye babes." Edward kissed her, then left.

Ten

Sindi returned from her meeting, which had been arranged for her by her art dealer friend, feeling on top of the world. She had managed to clinch a donation of a priceless painting as the main prize for Edward's charity ball auction. The day may have started off with her feeling uncertain and insecure about her relationship with Edward but after her talk and the lovemaking session with him she felt as if she was floating on air. Edward was turning out to be an adventurous lover but she liked it; she had liked it when he had made her look at herself as she was climaxing. It had been so … erotic. When Farranah saw Sindi walk in, she jumped up from her desk and followed her. Sindi looked at her enquiringly but the other woman simply grinned at her. As Sindi entered the main office, all her colleagues looked up at her with excitement. Even Aggie, the tea lady came out of the kitchen. Perplexed, Sindi continued towards her desk at the far side of the office, just in front of the accountant's office. When she reached it she saw why everyone was acting strange. On her chair sat a long white box with a black velvet ribbon wrapped around it. Everyone including Paula and the accountant gathered around her desk to see what was in the box.

"Come on, open the box already," Paula urged.

Sindi picked up the box and put it on top of the files and

papers on her desk and opened it. A small card sat on top of silver tissue paper. She picked it up and read it:

> *I know you can dress yourself; after all that is how you caught my attention. But I was driving past a shop when something in the window caught my attention. I could not help thinking how beautiful you would look wearing it. Please wear it tonight.*
> *B*

Sindi smiled to herself. She was chuffed he had taken the time to write the card and apparently choose the gift himself. This meant he put the package together, which made it all the more special.

"Come on already, we don't care about the card. Open the gift!" Farranah said.

Sindi laughed.

"OK, OK."

She pulled the tissue paper apart. Inside the box there were a neatly folded two-tone dress and a pair of strappy high-heeled sandals below the dress. On top of the dress was another box, black and small, with the name of an exclusive jeweller embossed on the lid in silver. Sindi picked up the box and opened it.

"Aaaaahhhhh ...," they all gasped in unison. Inside the small box glittered a diamond and tanzanite bracelet and matching three-tier teardrop diamond earrings. With a shaky hand Sindi picked up the bracelet, held it to the light and watched the beautiful array of colours dance and sparkle.

"Yoh! I bet those are real diamonds eh?" Sonet said.

"Jurre! I've never seen real diamonds up close! I have to brag about it to my mother. She will never believe me," Farranah added.

Excited, Sindi's attention moved to the other goodies in the box. She took the long elegant dress out and held it against her body. The cream silk bodice had a V neck in the front and back. The pleated skirt was made out of navy chiffon. Next she took out one of the sandals. It had a silver pointed heel and blue straps around the ankle and across the toes and a silver one that ran diagonally across the foot.

"Are these from Edward?" Paula asked.

"Yes."

"My, it seems the man is really trying to win your heart."

"And has good taste," someone else commented.

"He won me over long ago," Sindi said smiling.

"Why do wealthy men always court women with clothes and diamonds? It's so clichéd. It reeks Richard Gere circa 1990 in *Pretty Woman*," Katherine commented.

Farranah whispered to Sindi, "Ignore her. She's just jealous her husband is an ordinary data analyst and that she's no longer Paula's favourite – you are. Edward's event will bring in the most money any single event ever has in this company."

Sindi followed Farranah's advice and ignored Katherine's comment, as did everyone else. She allowed her colleagues to ooh and aah a bit longer, before she packed everything away. As her colleagues went back to work, Paula asked to see her in her office. Sindi followed Paula to her office. Inside, Paula closed the door and smiled to put Sindi at ease. She gestured for Sindi to sit. Sindi sat in one of the client chairs in front of Paula's desk. Paula chose the second chair and twisted it to face Sindi.

"Sindi, my dear, don't worry it's nothing serious. I just wanted to talk to you in private. I realise that you are the reason that Edward chose our small firm to plan his charity event. You have been with us for just under a year and in that time you have proven your worth and have conducted yourself professionally at all times. So I have faith in you that you will be able to balance your private and professional relationship with him. All I request is that should there be trouble between you and Edward that might affect the project you let me know. Is that fair?"

"Yes, that's fair but I promise to keep my private life out of my professional life."

"I know you will," Paula replied, standing up, a sign that she was reassured.

Sindi also got up and left. On her way to her desk she thought about calling Edward and thanking him for his gift but she had a better idea.

***

The doors pinged open on the Boateng Group's executive floor. Sindi walked over to Lauren's desk. Thuli was with her, berating her it seemed, for the poor girl looked like she was about to burst into tears.

"Good afternoon," she greeted the two women.

Lauren's strained face looked up at her but before she could say anything Thuli snapped, "Edward won't be able to see you. He's busy with back-to-back meetings and you don't have an appointment."

"I know. I just need to talk to him for two minutes only – he won't mind."

Thuli straightened up and folded her arms.

"You can tell me and I'll pass it on or if you prefer you can e-mail him."

"Eh .... No. This is personal and I'd rather do it in person."

"Nice try, I won't fall for that again. I know he's employed you to plan an event for him. You're nothing more than another employee to him. Some friendly advice: you are not the first or the only one to vie for his affections. Let me save you a lot unnecessary trouble and heartache: Mr Boateng doesn't date his employees."

"So I guess you know all your hoping and wishing is in vain?"

"Excuse me?"

Before Sindi could answer, Edward appeared with four other men. One of the men recognised Sindi. He smiled and waved at her. Sindi smiled and waved back. Edward turned to see who Shawn was waving at. When he saw it was Sindi he beckoned her over. Sindi eyed Thuli and went over to the men.

"Sindi – right?" Shawn drawled, hugging her.

"Yes. And you are ... Shawn?" she replied, surprised by the hug.

Shawn laughed. "Good memory. I haven't seen you since New Year's Eve. How are you?"

"Very well, thank you."

Sindi turned to greet Hermann.

"Ms Sindi, how are you?"

"I'm fine, thank you. It's so nice to see you. How is Grace?"

"She is well. She's arriving later this afternoon. She is looking forward to seeing you again."

Edward put his arm around her and pulled her to his side.

"Baby, meet Donald Spacey and Mohale Diale. Gentlemen, this is my beautiful other half, Sindi. They, along with Hermann and Shawn, are my partners in that deal we are celebrating tonight."

"Guess I'll be seeing you tonight then?" Sindi said smiling at the men.

The elevator arrived again.

"Yes, you will," Shawn answered.

The four men said their farewells and went down the elevator.

Edward turned to Sindi. "I'm sorry, babe, but I only have about twenty minutes before my next meeting."

"That's alright. That's plenty of time," Sindi said with a wicked glint in her eyes. "I just wanted to thank you for my beautiful gift."

A naughty grin spread over Edward's face. "Well, then, in that case why don't you step into my office," he said pulling her towards his office.

Sindi winked triumphantly at the seething Thuli before she disappeared down the passage with Edward.

***

"You look beautiful, friend, and the food tastes divine, as usual," Lulu gushed.

Sindi sighed. "Thank you. I don't know why but I was very nervous about tonight. I've done dozens of these events - in fact I've done bigger ones - but I was still nervous."

"Maybe it has to do with the fact you're the hostess tonight?" Lulu's voice carried a question.

"What? What are you talking about? Edward is hosting – I'm just the caterer."

Lulu exchanged her empty champagne glass for a fresh one from a passing waiter.

"I can't believe you," Lulu said. "I thought we were friends, *best* friends!"

"We are. You are my sister, there's no-one closer to me than you."

"Then why did I find out from that classless, tactless, rhino of a woman Lerato that you and Edward have been an item for a while now?" The hurt was evident in Lulu's eyes. "Apparently you two have been spotted out and about acting like two lovestruck teens," Lulu pouted.

"I don't even know who this classless, tactless, hippopotamus of a woman is!"

"I said rhino not hippo; she's not only fat she also has a huge horn in the middle of her head. If you're going to quote me you can at least do it properly."

"It's called paraphrasing: restating a statement using other words," Sindi said.

Lulu and Sindi burst out laughing.

"Stop it. You are not allowed to make me laugh. I'm mad and hurt."

Sindi hugged her friend. "Oh, friend. I'm sorry I didn't tell you sooner. It's just that I didn't want to tell you until I was sure about what was happening between us. Forgive me?"

"Only if you give me the scoop. Have you sinned yet?"

Sindi grinned naughtily. "Yes."

"Full scoop! When? Where? What happened? How was it?"

"OK, OK but somewhere private," Sindi answered pulling Lulu up the stairs. Sindi was about to open the first bedroom they came to, which happened to be the master bedroom, when she heard Edward's voice.

"...What? When?" his shocked voice carried clearly.

An inaudible female voice answered. Sindi's heart filled with dread. She signalled to Lulu to keep quiet. The two women pressed their ears to the door.

Edward's incredulous voice sounded again.

"How? What happened?"

The woman was weeping.

"I don't know what happened. I was napping and then I woke up in excruciating pain and needing to pee very badly. I could barely walk to the bathroom because of the painful cramps but when I finally made it nothing came out, even though my bladder felt full. So I went and got myself a glass of water thinking that would stimulate my bladder, and I took some painkillers." The woman sniffed hard. "My bladder felt full again. I was in so much pain I could only crawl back to the bathroom. As I lifted myself onto the toilet seat I felt something warm trickle down my leg and thought pee had escaped. As I was peeing I saw it was blood running down my legs. Just as I was getting over that shock I heard something drop in the water. Obviously I got up to see a-a-and … and … and …" Another hard sniff. "A-a-a-nd …" She tried again but instead wept uncontrollably. Sindi heard movement and shhh-ing sounds, and guessed Edward was consoling the woman.

Lulu tapped Sindi's shoulder.

"Who is she?" she whispered.

"I don't know," Sindi answered, worry weighing her heart down. Instinctively she knew whoever the woman was and whatever was going on spelled trouble for her.

"She sounds familiar," Lulu commented almost to herself.

The woman continued wailing. "Oh Edward! It was so terrible! All I saw was red water and blood all over the place, then ... th-th-then ... I saw him. I saw *our baby* floating in the toilet bowl!" A new wave of wails sounded.

Lulu gasped. She grabbed Sindi's shoulder gestured they should leave. A shocked and angry Sindi whispered, "You go, I want to hear more!"

The woman carried on, "I'm sorry to bother you like this but I didn't know who to turn to. You know I have no real friends in L.A. and how alone I feel there. I need you. Please, Edward. Don't make me go through this alone. I won't be able to. I know the foetus wasn't a proper baby yet but that was m-m-my baby, *our* baby. This is so traumatic for me. All I'm asking is that you be there for me. Please. You know the troubles I have and I want to stay away from the wrong path."

L.A.? Could this be Sasa? But how? They broke up two years ago. How could she have been pregnant with his baby? Sindi remembered Edward's recent trip to the U.S.A. *He was gone for three weeks – that's more than enough time to make a baby. But that trip was for business and he went to Chicago. Yeah, but people travel between cities all the time.* Sindi closed her eyes and shook her thoughts away.

"Shhh ... shhh ... Of course I'll be there for you. I'll always be there for you when you need me," Edward promised.

Always? Sindi had heard enough. She straightened up and ran for the stairs. Lulu chased after her.

"*Tshomi!*"

Sindi spun around. "Let's first hear what he has to say," Sindi said unconvincingly before spinning around again and running down the stairs. Lulu let her go.

Sindi hid in one of the guest toilets until she felt composed enough to deal with people. It was going to be harder now to deal with the curious stares and probing questions. It seemed everyone at the party was on a mission to find out if the rumours of her relationship with Edward were true or not. She wished she hadn't gone upstairs, hadn't listened in. *It's true; ignorance is bliss and what is it that they say about hindsight and foresight again? Hindsight is the mother of foresight? Well, even if I just made that up, it should be a saying. None of this makes sense ... But of course! Sasa must have had the miscarriage two years ago,* she thought, trying to reassure herself. *That's why she left and that's why Edward said he'll always be there for her. She must have come back because she's still not over what happened and needs to find closure.* Feeling better, Sindi stood and tidied herself up in the mirror before returning to the party.

Edward was busy making a speech when she came out of the toilet. A wide smile spread on his face when he spotted her.

"... and so the Boateng Group is very excited to announce the expansion of its operations. A few gold deposits were discovered near the old Yellow Mines near Soweto. Further investigation has determined the mines aren't as dry as previously thought – there is more gold to be found if we drill further down."

An excited murmur erupted amongst the guests.

Edward carried on, "In this venture I am joined by Iranium Inc., a Chicago-based engineering firm, the Spacey Trust, which owns the land, and investors Hermann Awola and Mohale Diale. It is a very exciting project we are about to embark on. One that will revitalise the economy, bringing much needed jobs to the impoverished communities surrounding the mine. An official press briefing and launch where we will detail the scope of the project will be held, but we wanted you to be the first to know, since you are our closest friends. "

There was enthusiastic applause. Edward raised his hand to signal silence.

"OK I get it. You want me to stop talking." Everyone laughed. "Before I step down I want to thank a very special woman in my life, Miss Sindi Mali. She organised this fabulous soirée and prepared all the food. She caters small private functions so I suggest you all get her details. Baby," Edward raised his glass to her. Everyone's eyes turned to her, and Sindi felt her face become hot with embarrassment. "Thank you and congratulations on a successful evening. Now you may clap."

Everyone laughed and clapped.

Lulu came up behind Sindi and grabbed her elbow,

pulling her aside. "Remember when I said the woman who was speaking to Edward in the bedroom has a familiar voice?"

Sindi nodded.

Lulu sighed. "Well, that's because it was Sasa."

Sindi felt ice freeze over her heart as Lulu confirmed what she suspected.

"She's still here. There she is – talking to Duma."

Sindi looked in the direction Lulu pointed to. She saw a tall, elegant, woman throwing her head back in laughter at whatever Duma was saying. She looked bold and beautiful as if she were ready to conquer the world. Every movement she made was poised and graceful – there was no trace of the vulnerable, crying woman she'd been a mere ten minutes ago.

"Gorgeous dress," Sindi commented jealously.

"She has always been on point, shame." Lulu winced as she realised what she just said. "Sorry, friend, I know you don't need to know that but it is the truth."

"No, I do need to hear it. The truth is the truth and I need to know what I'm up against."

Sindi looked at the beautiful woman again, taking in her red long-sleeved floor-length dress and diamond earrings and bracelet. Even her small clutch bag sparkled. Her long, pin-straight, glossy weave was pulled to one side and cascaded over her right shoulder, leaving her bare back fully exposed. Sindi knew she paled next to this gorgeous woman. The cream and navy dress Edward had bought her lost its appeal all of a sudden. *She certainly doesn't mind attracting attention or else she wouldn't have worn such a bold colour. I wonder if Edward bought her that jewellery and did he give her an invite?* Suddenly Sindi couldn't wait for everyone to leave. She had questions and needed answers.

"She's really beautiful," she finally admitted.

Lulu looked at her sharply. "So are you. And don't forget you're the one Edward acknowledged tonight and you're the one he'll be laying his head next to tonight."

Sindi's insecurities flooded back. "Yeah, but till when?" she mumbled under her breath but not loudly enough for Lulu to hear her. "You're truly a good friend," she said out loud.

"Squeeze me if you mean it," Lulu said in a teasing voice, knowing her friend needed a hug but would be too proud to accept one.

Sindi laughed as she opened her arms for the embrace.

"Lulu, don't you have a partner to monopolise instead of mine?" Edward's warm playful voice broke the two women's embrace.

"Now, now, Edward. Jealousy is such a nasty thing; don't hate me just because she has more love for me," Lulu teased back.

"Not for much longer if I have anything to do with it," Edward returned, pulling Sindi into a soft kiss.

"Let me go find my husband and beg for a kiss of my own," Lulu said, smiling and walking away.

Edward laughed. Edward slid a hand around her waist and the other captured her hand. He started to sway her to the music.

"Did I tell you that you look absolutely amazing, gorgeous, exceptionally beautiful, incredible, stunning, graceful, sexy and adorable?" Edward said, dipping her and nuzzling her neck.

Sindi smiled lightly and from her bent position she saw Sasa staring at them with a tight mouth. Edward pulled her back up.

"My, that's quite a list of adjectives. I'm flattered."

"It's all true and that's just a fraction of the words I could use to describe the beautiful, incredible woman you are. I'm forever indebted to all the losers who allowed you to slip away." Edward pulled her closer then kissed her deeply.

***

Sindi and Edward had just walked back into the penthouse, with their arms wrapped around each other, after bidding farewell to their last guests when they saw Sasa descending down the stairs yawning.

"Oh my! Am I the last guest? How embarrassing," she giggled self-consciously.

Edward smiled at her. "Yes, you are."

Sasa reached the last stair and towered above them.

"I must have napped longer than I intended. I hope you don't mind but I took the liberty of taking a nap upstairs.

I guess it's only now that the jet lag is hitting me."

"Of course not," Sindi said after she finally found her voice. Her annoyance hid behind her eyes. *If you were tired why didn't you just go home?*

Sasa flashed Sindi a bright smile.

"Hello, I'm Sasa Dlamini," she introduced herself and offered Sindi her hand.

Sindi reluctantly took it and forced a smile.

"Sindi Mali," she answered. She leaned closer in to Edward after Sasa dropped her hand, more for security than territory. Edward held her tighter.

Sasa's astute eyes caught the action.

"Well, I guess I must get going. I'm sure you two are tired." Sasa's friendly smile was still plastered on her face. "Well done on tonight and the food was absolutely amazing."

"Thank you," Sindi replied.

"Do you have transport home?" Edward asked.

"No, I was going to ask reception to give me a taxi number."

"Where are you staying?"

"I'm booked in a hotel in the CBD."

"I'll take you," Edward said climbing the stairs to fetch his car keys.

"Oh no! I couldn't ask you to do that," Sasa protested.

"It's no problem." Edward looked at Sindi. "You don't mind do you, babe?"

Sindi shook her head.

"In that case, thank you to you both." Sasa flashed another bright smile.

"Good night, Sasa. It was nice meeting you," Sindi said, following Edward up the stairs.

In the bedroom Edward grabbed his car key and gave her a peck. "I'll be back soon."

Sindi prepared for bed. She washed her face and brushed her teeth and then climbed into bed with a lump in her throat.

***

Edward climbed into bed behind Sindi. Her eyes flashed open immediately and searched in the darkness for the time on the alarm clock beside the bed. Edward had been gone for an hour. The lump in her throat turned into a rock. Edward gently stroked her. Sindi stilled herself. Edward slid closer, pressing himself against her backside.

"Baby," he whispered.

Sindi shut her eyes and willed her body to stop betraying her.

"Baby," he repeated.

She felt her nipples respond to his stroking. Edward tried one more time to wake her up, before giving up and just holding her tight. Finally the hot tears she had been holding back for the hour Edward had been gone fell silently onto her pillow.

Eleven

"Morning, babe," Edward smiled brightly as Sindi walked into the kitchen.

Sindi croaked her reply with a yawn and then slumped onto a stool at the breakfast nook.

"Are you feeling OK? You don't sound well and your eyes are red and slightly puffy."

Sindi cleared her throat. "I must be coming down with something. I'll get something from the pharmacy to nip it in the bud."

"I'll ask Francis to organise it for you."

Edward picked up the tray he was setting and placed it in front of her. He dropped a kiss on her forehead. "I was going to serve you breakfast in bed but, alas, you had to wake up." He picked up his plate and sat next to her.

"Thanks." Sindi's voice, although still gruff, sounded better. She looked at her beautifully presented plate.

"I noticed you prefer a light breakfast so I made this," Edward explained.

"Looks delicious. What is it?" She asked, looking at the two roll halves on her plate with sunny-side up eggs in the centre, garnished with rocket leaves.

"All-in-one breakfast. Hollowed rolls filled with a tomato, egg and feta relish; all baked in the oven."

Sindi lifted one crunchy roll and bit into it. "Mmmm ... this is good."

"Glad you like it," Edward said, crunching into his own roll.

They ate in silence for a while. Then Sindi decided to bite the bullet and broach the subject of the cause of her restless night. She moistened her throat with a sip of her juice.

"You came back pretty late last night," she commented as nonchalantly as she could.

Edward swallowed and put his half-eaten roll back on the plate.

"Yeah, I did. Sasa needed someone to talk to so I stayed and talked to her for a while."

"In her hotel room?"

"Yes."

"I see." Sindi took another bite. This time it felt like she was chewing concrete.

Edward's hand covered her left hand, which was resting on the counter.

"Nothing happened. We just talked."

"About?" The concrete went down to her stomach with a sickening thud and became dead weight.

Edward shrugged and went back to his meal.

"She's going through something and needs a friend right now."

"I see." Sindi got up and went to the sink to rinse her plate and then put it in the dishwasher. Edward polished his plate off as well and did the same. When he was done, Edward took her hands in his and pulled her back to the breakfast nook to sit down.

"I need to talk to you about something."

"What is it?" she asked.

Edward shifted in his seat uncomfortably.

"Sasa miscarried my baby."

"Is that why you two broke up? Was it because of the miscarriage?" Sindi asked hopefully.

Edward squirmed. "No. We … I … the miscarriage was recent."

Sindi's heart dipped and her world fell off its axis. She was quiet for a while as her mind raced to make sense of what he'd just said.

"How recent?"

Edward looked like he wished he didn't have to answer her.

"It happened five days ago."

"F-five days ago! That was now-now! How far along was she?"

Embarrassment covered Edward's face.

"Four weeks."

Shock and then anger passed over Sindi. She snatched her hands away and jumped off the stool.

"You lied to me! You told me there was only me!"

"No, baby, I did not lie to you."

"If she was four weeks pregnant that means you slept with her very recently. Four weeks ago you were in the US. Is that when you slept with her?"

Edward nodded silently.

Sindi's face contorted in disgust. "Then you came straight back to me and I foolishly welcomed you with open arms. Talk about having a girl in every city," she said, before stomping out of the kitchen.

Edward chased after her. He caught up with her just before she reached the stairs.

"Sindi, baby, it wasn't like that. Sasa was a one-off, a mistake. I even told her afterwards that I've met someone I really like and that I was pursuing you. And please remember you and I were not in a relationship at the time. You were still chasing me away." He held on to her hand.

"Still, you slept with another woman while pursuing me. How can I be sure that your feelings for me are sincere? I can't do this; I'm leaving." She snatched her hand away from his and went up the stairs.

When she returned she was dressed and had her bag in her hand. Edward was waiting for her at the foot of the stairs.

"Please give me a chance to explain. Afterwards I will take you home. Just allow me to explain, please," he begged.

"Fine," Sindi relented, desperate for a reason to listen to the voice that was being drowned out by logic, the voice that was begging her to not walk away, the part of her that still yearned for him. She left her bag at the foot of the stairs and walked to the lounge and sat down. Edward followed and sat opposite her.

"I have a confession to make," he began. "My trip to the States was not only about business. Actually I was only in Chicago for a day as negotiations had been done long ago and it was a matter of formalising everything."

Sindi held back a snide comment.

Edward continued, "When Sasa and I broke up she decided to pursue her dream of becoming a Hollywood actress so she moved to L.A. As you know her industry is cut-throat and it can be very hard to get your foot in the door."

"OK, but what does that have to do with you impregnating her?"

"When we broke up two years ago I gave her a little bit of money to keep her going till she found her feet. But unfortunately things didn't go very well for her there; she wasn't getting any jobs, she made the wrong friends and her money began to run out. She became depressed and stressed and started drinking heavily, and her new friends introduced her to drugs."

"I still don't see what that has to do with you sleeping with her. What, you felt sorry for her so you decided to comfort her between the sheets?"

"No. The week before my trip I received a desperate call from her – she was hysterical and crying, she said she was a mess. I was due in the States so I decided to incorporate seeing her into my trip. I flew in a couple of days before I was scheduled to just so I could see her. When I got there she was in really bad state, said she was coming down from a high." Edward looked at Sindi desperately, pleading for her to understand. "She's a friend who was in trouble and needed my help so I enrolled her in an out-patient programme. The night before I flew to Chicago she was emotionally vulnerable, pleading with me not to go. I was consoling her and then she started kissing me. Before I knew it, one thing led to another and we ended up in bed together. It was a mistake. I know I shouldn't have done it but I hadn't been with a woman ever since I met you on Christmas Day and I had all this pent-up sexual tension from you, I was weak – I succumbed. My meeting was Friday then I returned to L.A. the following day. I wanted to make sure she was alright and that's why I extended my trip. I swear we made love that one time only. We are just friends and nothing more."

"No, you're not just friends. This woman was an integral part of your life for almost a decade. I don't know how to feel about this. I understand you helping her and I know we weren't an official couple then, but I can't help feeling betrayed."

"Baby, I can't tell you how sorry I am. I regret what I did."

"Is she back for good?"

"I don't know. She fell pregnant but had a miscarriage. She's asked for my support and because she is fragile at the moment I want to be there for her. I don't want her to turn to alcohol or drugs."

Sindi thought of the tall, confident woman she had seen last night. *She sure did not look fragile last night.* Finally logic won the battle but the small voice of hope wasn't willing to give up without a fight.

"I know,' she confessed. "I overheard you two talking last night."

Edward went to sit next to her and hugged her. "Oh, baby, I'm sorry you had to find out like that. Please don't let this come between us."

"I'm not ending us, I just need some space. What's happening right now is unexpected."

"Alright," he conceded, standing up. "I'll take you home."

"No, it's fine. I'll take a taxi."

"Take my sister's car; no-one is using it."

Sindi didn't really want to take his sister's car as that would leave the door between them open. But then again she didn't really want to close the door now, did she? She took the car key and murmured her thanks.

***

"Yoh! You look terrible!" was the first thing Farranah said when Sindi walked into the office on Monday morning. *Jeez, Farranah, how about some tact? I know I look horrible but there's no need to tell the whole world!* It was true. Sindi herself had been surprised by the face that had greeted her in the mirror that morning. Her eyes were red and swollen and her nose felt as if it had been sanded because of all the crying she'd been doing over the weekend. She had admitted to herself as she had stared at her hideous face that watching romantic films over and over again and listening to Wilson, Paul and Eddie yesterday had not been the brightest of ideas. *But come on, what better way is there to torture yourself about your pathetic love life than listening to the famous, "I'm just a boy standing in front of a girl asking her to love him" line? And of course romance woes are incomplete without the Metro FM trio and their Sunday R&B playlist to give you hope about everlasting love and at the same time remind you how lonely you are.* Sindi's mind came back to the present.

"Morning to you too, Farranah," she said.

"And you sound terrible. What's wrong?"

"Allergies," Sindi replied.

"Are you sure you shouldn't be resting?"

"No, I took medication." The last thing Sindi wanted to do was sit at home with only her thoughts for company.

"OK, there's an impromptu staff meeting. The others are already in the boardroom," Farranah said.

Sindi went to the boardroom. Her other colleagues also showed concern but she told them the same thing she'd told Farranah. Paula needed more assurance than the others but eventually she also gave up trying to convince her to go home. After the meeting she went straight to her desk, while her colleagues either went for a smoke break or went to the kitchen to make themselves coffee. She fired up her computer and watched as her inbox updated with new mail. At a glance she saw she had several from Lulu and one from Edward. She opened the last e-mail from Lulu:

OK, I give up now. If you don't call me by 10.15 (Farranah told me by 10 o'clock your meeting will be over) I shall have no option but to call the police and report you as a missing person (you have been MIA for 48 hrs now) and I will also contact Khumbul'ekhaya. (Your least flatering pic will be on TV and Andile will be like: Have you seen this woman? She was last seen on Saturday morning, 12 February, wearing blue jeans and a black top. Sindi, Sisi, goduka uyakhunjulw'ekhaya).
xo Lu.

Sindi rolled her eyes at Lulu's melodramatic e-mail but nonetheless she found herself giggling. She clicked Edward's e-mail open. It contained a slide with a "*click here to play*" link. She clicked the link and her screen suddenly exploded to a huge heart and smaller multicoloured hearts rained around the big red one. Text flew to the big heart:

Happy Valentine's Day to my favourite girl.

The heart suddenly morphed and an animation of a boy giving a girl a rose and the girl kissing the boy played, then the next screen said:

Will you please be my Valentine?

Again, Sindi found herself giggling. *How cheesy.* She saw the time on the corner of her computer screen, 10.10. She decided to call Lulu: she was crazy enough to honour her threat. She fished in her bag for her phone and switched it on. More messages flooded in – mostly from Lulu and Edward. Lulu managed to beat Edward by one message. Sindi went to make the call in Edward's sister's car for privacy. She dialled Lulu's number. The phone rang once before Lulu answered.

"Finally! I was about to call the police!"

"You are so full of drama. How does Duma handle you?"

"Never mind about Duma, how are you? Duma told me what happened. He says Edward is going out of his mind. The guy is so desperate he even came to me but obviously, even though I think you should give him a second chance, I had your back and told him he was a typical stupid male person. But tshomz, I really think you should give him a second chance. He is so worth it," Lulu rushed in.

"May I speak now?"

Lulu laughed. "Yes. You may."

"I didn't break up with him. I just needed time and space to decide what I truly want and what I'm willing to tolerate. I'm done with heartbreak; I'm only willing to put myself out there if I'm satisfied his intentions are true and sincere. If things don't work out it must be because they just didn't work, not because he was making a fool of me."

"Fair enough, I can respect that." Someone interrupted Lulu. "Listen, friend, I have to go. Please don't hide yourself, ne? Love you and will call you tonight.

Mwhaah!" With that Lulu hung up. Sindi stared at the receiver, then shook her head and went back to the office.

An hour later, a smiling Farranah walked up to her desk carrying a huge white teddy holding a red heart that said *Happy Valentine's Day* and a bouquet of a dozen perfect long-stemmed red roses. Sindi laughed as she accepted the gifts, which reminded her of high school. *Wow, Cardies still sells these teddies?* She removed the handwritten card stuck in the flowers and read:

> *Old school worked to win your heart*
> *Hoping old school will help win your*
> *forgiveness ...*
> *Roses are red*
> *Violets are blue*
> *You drive me mad*
> *I hope I drive you mad too*
> *Please be my Valentine (you never replied to my e-mail)* ☹

See? He always takes the time to write his own cards. He cares about you, give him a chance. Logic told her to pick up her skirts and run as fast as she could but a strong part of her urged her to do otherwise. Her inner being longed for Edward. Sindi decided she would take the risk and if she turned out to be wrong then she would give up on ever finding her Prince Charming. After all nowadays, with sperm banks and all, it was possible for her to fulfil her dream of having a child one day without having a man beside her. And she was capable of raising her child and creating a home for her and her child alone. She decided to take an early lunch to do some shopping. She went to Clicks and bought a Valentine's Day themed coffee mug and the cheesiest Hallmark card and wrapping paper she could find. After much hunting she finally found two pairs of boxers: one was red with white hearts and the other was white with red hearts. On her way back to the office she went past a gift shop and bought a small box. Sitting in the car she neatly rolled the boxers and put them in the mug, and then she placed the mug and card in the box. She drove back to the office. She took the box and wrapping paper in with her. At her desk, she scribbled a message in the card:

Roses are red
Violets are blue
I'm into you
Like you are into me
Yes, I will be your Valentine
xo Sindi M

Sindi wished she could be there to see the look on his face when he opened his gift. She slipped the card in with the mug and wrapped the box. Then she called a courier company to deliver the gift. An hour later another gift was delivered to her: this time a single stem with a note attached:

Kiss captured ☺☺☺
You have just made my day!
Roses are red
Violets are blue
You put the sunshine in my heart
Be ready for me at 7.30pm
I know that does not rhyme
But I do not care

xoxo
E

P.S. Pack an overnight bag and dress to impress.

Twelve

Sindi's heart jumped as she opened her door and saw Edward standing there with a smile on his face and a huge bouquet of red and pink roses. She soaked in his beauty in his burgundy suit and blue shirt, a look finished off with a pink handkerchief in his suit pocket. The top buttons of his shirt were unbuttoned, reminding her of their fateful meeting. She couldn't decide if he complemented the ensemble or if it was the ensemble that complemented him. Sindi was pleased with her choice of outfit. It suited his very well. She had decided on a navy blue, figure hugging, strapless knee-length dress with a sweet-heart neckline. Her waist was clinched with a gold cuff belt and a deep burgundy and red earrings dangled from her ears. She finished the look with a pair of burgundy, pointed-toe snake-skin stilettos and a maroon and gold clutch bag. Her hair was loose. Edward let out a long whistle.

"Happy Valentine's Day, babe; you look stunning." He engulfed her in a kiss, then picked her up and kicked the door closed.

Sindi blushed. She was grateful the potato remedy for puffy eyes had worked and her eyes were back to normal.

"You have no idea how frantic I've been this past weekend not knowing whether or not I'd lost you," he continued.

"Well, if this is the response I get for not seeing you for just two days I wonder what kind of reception I would get if I didn't see you for a week."

"Don't you dare!" Edward growled before nuzzling her neck.

Sindi laughed and Edward set her down.

"Let me quickly finish packing my overnight bag, then we can go," she said turning around and going to the bedroom. Edward followed her and sat on the bed as she collected things.

"It seems we had a telepathic exchange when we got dressed. What are the chances we'd end up in outfits that coordinate? Sindi joked as she quickly packed her bag. Edward reached out to Sindi and pulled her onto his lap.

"I don't know why you insist on ignoring the blatant fact that you and I are twin souls." He kissed her slowly. "Two souls that make a great whole." He gave her a peck before gently pushing her off him, zipping her overnight bag and picking it up.

"Come on, let's go. I can't wait to spoil you this evening."

Sindi smiled in anticipation and picked up her clutch bag from the bed before slipping her hand into Edward's outstretched hand.

"Are you going to give me a clue about tonight?" she asked as they walked out.

"You're going to have to be patient," he answered.

"Mmm, thought as much."

***

As they neared the V&A Waterfront, Sindi turned to Edward.

"Are we going to your place?" she asked with some disappointment.

Edward smiled at her tone. "I told you, you are going to have to be patient."

"Okay," Sindi replied, trying hard to hide her feelings. Although she hadn't had any specific expectation, dinner at home was not something she had anticipated, especially since his card had alluded to something special. Her disenchantment deepened as Edward pulled into his penthouse parking lot. She couldn't believe he had made her dress up for nothing.

"Are you disappointed, babe?" He asked as they got out of the car. Edward went to the boot to get her bag out. He reached for her hand.

"No, I was just asking." Sindi squeezed his hand, "As long as we are together, I'm happy."

"I think you are disappointed. If I promise to fix your disappointment, will you smile?"

Sindi let out a small laugh and a smile. "I'm not disappointed, I promise!"

"Honest?"

"Honest."

"No, I don't like you like this. Let's see if I can do something about it." Edward turned to the exit, pulling her with him, as if it were a last minute decision.

"Where are we going?"

"Out. I've disappointed you, I'm going to make it up to you."

"OK, but shouldn't we leave the bag behind?"

Edward shrugged and swung the bag over his shoulder suspiciously.

"Nah, it's not heavy so it's not bothering me."

"Are we going to walk?" she asked testing him.

"Why not? The weather is gorgeous," he let go of her hand and took out his phone to text.

Sindi's suspicion that he was up to something was confirmed.

"Well, Mr Beautiful Weather, so long as you don't forget I'm wearing heels. The amount of walking I can do is limited," Sindi answered, her heart now smiling.

"Don't worry, if your feet get tired I'll carry you." Edward led them to where the *Afia* was berthed.

"Are we going on a trip?" Sindi asked.

Edward growled good-naturedly. "You do realise you make surprising you a challenge?"

Sindi giggled. "OK, no more questions."

When they reached the *Afia*, Nick, Kelly and another crew member were waiting for them. Nick was wearing his captain's uniform. Kelly was dressed formally while the other crew member was wearing a black server's uniform.

"Good evening Mr Boateng," Nick said holding out his hand.

"Good evening captain," Edward replied shaking Nick's hand. "Ms Rauls, Siya." Edward nodded at the other two as he acknowledged them.

"Good evening sir," they replied in unison and smiled at Sindi who smiled back.

"Ms Mali, it is a pleasure to see you again," Nick said.

"Thank you captain, it's a pleasure to see you too."

"Siya, can you please take Ms Mali's bag?" Edward said, handing over the overnight bag.

"Yes sir," Siya replied taking the bag.

"We are ready to set sail to Langebaan at any moment sir," Nick said. "Club Mykonos Resort has also agreed for us to berth there."

"Everything is arranged?"

"Yes sir, the only thing we have been waiting for is the two of you," Kelly answered with a smile.

"Well then there's no more reason to wait." Edward put his hand on the small of Sindi's back and guided her inside the yacht. It was after 8pm and the sky was starting to darken. When they entered, the yacht's splendour took Sindi's breath away, again. The yacht was bathed in a warm glow and a trail of hot pink and pale pink rose petals led to the deck outside where a formal table was laid. The dinnerware and crystal glasses glistened creating an ambience of cultured elegance. At the centrepiece, small candles were laid out in a zigzag pattern and a mass of deep red rose petals surrounded them. Siya stood by the table, with a bottle of champagne in an ice bucket chilling next to him. As soon as Edward and Sindi stepped out the five-man band started playing a soul-jazz number. The lead singer's voice was deep, strong and melodious; the way Sindi like her male voices to be. Edward led Sindi to the table and pulled out her chair for her and then quickly went to sit in his.

"Thank you," she smiled as she sat down. A jeweller's box sat on her under plate, on top of the typed four-course menu. Sindi looked up in surprise and embarrassment. "I'm sorry I didn't get you anything. I didn't realise you were going to get me another present."

Edward reached for her hands across the table. "You being here with me and forgiving me is the best gift I could ever ask for. I love you, Sindi Mali, and I never want to lose you."

Sindi's heart soared. She couldn't believe he had said those special three words. And what better moment could he have chosen than this one, on the day of celebrating love?

"Hearing you tell me you love me is the best gift I could ever ask for. I love you too, Edward Boateng, and I never want you to lose me."

Edward chuckled. "You are quite cheeky, Ms Mali. Come here," he said pulling her into a kiss.

Siya poured them champagne then discreetly disappeared.

"So did I make up for disappointing you?" Edward asked as he took a sip of his champagne.

Sindi burst out laughing. "I told you I wasn't disappointed!"

Edward chuckled. "And that's your story and you're sticking to it."

"Whatever. But seriously, had I been disappointed then yes this would have redeemed you."

Edward chuckled some more. "That's good to know. Now open your gift."

Sindi opened her gift.

"Oh wow, this is exquisite," she said holding the diamond and tanzanite necklace against her chest.

"It contrasts nicely with your earrings and bracelet."

"I absolutely love it," she said leaning over the table and kissing him again.

Sindi savoured each dish the chef had produced. By the time the three-hour trip to Langebaan was over Sindi and Edward were done with dinner and had moved to the long couch that curved with the railing at the stairs. The band was still playing. Sindi sat snuggled in Edward's arms, both drinking a strawberry champagne cocktail. The champagne made Sindi's head buzz nicely. She craved Edward's lovemaking desperately. She lifted her head and pulled Edward's head to her lips.

"Ahem," Kelly interrupted. "Sir we've berthed."

"Did you book rooms for the whole crew and the band?"

"Yes sir."

"Good. You guys can go on ahead and book yourselves in. Have a good evening and please thank the rest of the crew for us. The evening was splendid."

Kelly smiled. "I'm glad sir. Good evening Ms Mali."

Sindi smiled back at her. "Good evening Ms Rauls."

Edward and Sindi could hear the crew chatter as they disembarked.

Edward turned to her. "We also have a room booked here but I'd rather spend the night with you here. If the idea of sleeping in a ya …"

Sindi put her hand over his mouth and kissed him. "I'd love to spend the night here. I've never slept in a yacht before and I've never made love in a yacht before," she said naughtily.

Edward stood up and lifted her up. "Well then, I guess I have some rectifying to do," he said taking her to the master cabin. They closed the evening with a very long, earth-shattering love-making session. Before falling asleep, Edward kissed her shoulder and whispered, "I love you, please never leave me."

The following morning Edward surprised her with breakfast in bed. After breakfast they made love again. The crew had the morning off so Edward and Sindi had time to themselves. They stayed in bed chatting, laughing and making out. Sasa did not even feature in any of their thoughts. Sindi was deliriously happy; she couldn't think of a single moment in her life that could compare to this moment – not even by a shade.

The next two weeks seemed to float by. Edward and Sindi fell into an easy intuitive pattern. Sindi felt like she had known him and been with him forever. Everything just felt right. It was as if she knew his soul. She could read him and he could read her. That was why she instinctively knew something was up when he had called her that Friday to ask her what time she'd be available for lunch. An unknown dread had filled her the moment she heard his voice on the other end of the line.

Sindi followed the maître d' to Edward's table. He stood up immediately. Sindi had seen him just that morning but he still managed to take her breath away. She admired his form in the pearl-grey suit he was wearing. Edward kissed her cheek before pulling out her chair for her. As soon as she was seated, a waiter appeared by her side and asked her if she wanted something to drink. Sindi noticed Edward was drinking whisky. *Whatever he wants to tell me must be quite serious if he is drinking during working hours.* She asked for a spritzer and the waiter disappeared. Edward asked her about her morning and talked about mundane things while she studied the menu. The dread inside her festered. Since she had little appetite she decided on the smoked chicken salad. The waiter returned with her spritzer and they placed their orders and the waiter disappeared again.

Unable to stand the suspense any longer, Sindi decided to tackle him head on.

"You're acting nervous, so how about just telling me what you want to tell me and get it over with?"

Edward looked at her anxiously before reaching for her hands and staring into her eyes.

"OK. Sasa came to see me at the office this morning.

She has decided to move back to South Africa. She can't afford to stay at her hotel indefinitely; she needs a place to stay until she finds a job and her own place."

*Doesn't this woman have family? She's South African, for crying out loud, and she spent many years living here in Cape Town. She must have at least **one** other friend she can lean on.*

"That can take quite a while," Sindi said quietly.

Edward squeezed her hands. "I know, baby, but she has nowhere else to go. Her family is in KwaZulu-Natal."

There you go! KwaZulu-Natal is a good option: sun, sand, sea and eternal summer.

"Most of her friends were friends we had made as a couple and she feels awkward asking them for help as she lost contact with them when we broke up."

Wasn't she a model at some time? How about her model friends?

Sindi forced a smile. "I know you want to help her. Your kind heart is one of the things I love about you and it says a lot that you care about her wellbeing even though you two broke up years ago. So it's OK with me."

Edward kissed her hands. "Thank you, baby. You have a generous heart. I know this can't be easy for you and I promise I won't make the same mistake twice. Anyway, you'll be around too."

Sindi simply smiled in response. Their food arrived. Sindi might as well have been eating air for all she could taste. She was too preoccupied with thoughts of the beautiful Sasa Dlamini and Edward living under the same roof. Sasa Dlamini, the woman he'd been so cut up over he hadn't dated any other woman seriously for two years after her. How she managed to handle the rest of the lunch she didn't know. She was just relieved to be back behind her desk; she needed work to distract her from her thoughts about Sasa.

***

Sindi was on the phone with Lulu while she was preparing snacks in Edward's kitchen for the DVD night she and Edward had decided on during lunch. Edward was to pick up the DVDs on the way home.

"... so seeing as you and Edward are now an official item it's only right that you should come to Hermanus with us. We have weekend-away trips every month and we each get a chance to choose a destination. It's fun and it gives us time to unwind away from our men. So are you in? Mind you, I'm only asking you as a formality. We all expect you to join us."

"Um ... who did you say is also coming on this trip?"

"All the other important WAGs. Now that you're unofficially "Mrs Edward Boateng" you will be socialising with them, so you might as well start now. And what better way to meet them than a nice relaxing weekend getaway?"

"I know you will not stop badgering me till I say yes so, yes, I'll come."

Lulu squealed in excitement. Sindi held the receiver

away from her ear, afraid that Lulu might burst her eardrum.

"Great! So, not next weekend but the one after the next."

"OK."

"Bye, my friend-o, we're gonna have so much fun-o at the resort-o!"

"Bye, Lulu," Sindi said chuckling at her crazy friend.

Sindi hung up the phone and pushed it into the back pocket of her jeans. She picked up the tray of snacks and took it to the TV room, placing it on the coffee table. She heard someone enter the penthouse and turned around with a smile. Her smile froze on her face as she stood facing the cause of her anxiety. As usual Sasa looked immaculate, managing to make Sindi feel below par in her well-fitting, distressed, designer pants and light tee. *How does she do it? How can one wear leather pants on a hot African summer's day and not only look stunning but as cool as a cucumber too?* Sindi still couldn't find a trace of vulnerability in this woman who exuded enough confidence to share with the entire world and still have more than enough left over for herself.

"Hello," Sasa said with a smile. "Sindi, right?"

"Ye-yes," Sindi cleared her throat.

"Did Edward tell you I shall be moving in with him?"

"Yes, we discussed it this afternoon," Sindi replied with more confidence.

Sasa smiled, but Sindi sensed malice behind her smile.

"Great, you know he was quick to suggest I move in with him. I bet you he misses living with a woman. So I'll just go choose my bedroom?"

Sindi had asked Mam'Sheila to prepare the farthest bedroom from the main bedroom, which was next to Edward's sister's room at the end of the hall.

"We've prepared the room right at the end of the hallway for you."

Something that resembled annoyance flitted across the other woman's face for a split second but it was so quick Sindi thought she'd imagined it.

"Thank you," Sasa said graciously. She started up the stairs, followed by Francis and the porter wrestling her Burberry luggage up the stairs after her.

Sindi pulled out her phone. Edward needed to come back home asap. She didn't know what she would chat to Sasa about and she was not up for awkward conversation. Just then Edward walked in carrying DVDs and a bottle of her favourite white wine. Sindi walked up to him and greeted him with a kiss.

"Guess who just moved in?" she said.

Edward's eyebrows shot up. "Sasa? I didn't expect her to move in so soon. Let me go welcome her."

"I'll open the bottle and I still need to make the popcorn," Sindi said taking the wine and DVDs.

By the time Edward came downstairs in his jeans, Sindi had already popped the first DVD in the player and was sipping on the wine.

"I invited her to join us. I hope you don't mind," Edward said as he sat down beside her.

"Of course not," Sindi lied.

***

By the time her weekend away with the other wives and girlfriends arrived Sindi was so grateful that Lulu had made her tag along. It meant she would get a break from Sasa. She didn't know if she was imagining things but she sensed that Sasa was pushing her aside every chance she got. It was more than enough that somehow Sasa managed to involve herself in every plan Sindi and Edward made, let alone that Sasa always managed to manipulate everything to be about her and Edward and their history together. At times Sindi could sense Edward was uncomfortable and when he saw she was unhappy he would change the topic or situation to include her. He tried as much as he could to assure her of his love but she couldn't help feeling Sasa was on a mission. She felt deeply threatened. After all, she and Edward didn't have a history as rich as the one he shared with Sasa. Then there was the fact he had been so heartbroken after she'd left that he hadn't been able to date any other woman seriously. Moments alone with Edward, save for bed time and their lunch dates, were a rarity with Sasa around all the time.

As fun and relaxing as the weekend away in Hermanus was, Lulu could see something was troubling her friend.

During the long drive home she cornered Sindi. Sindi broke down and told Lulu her suspicions and fear. An angry Lulu pulled to the side of the road and comforted her.

"What a bitch! You know, I've never really liked that woman. I wouldn't put anything past her. Girlfriend, you have to fight for your man! You can't roll over and hand him over to her on a silver platter!" Lulu chastised. "Don't think for a minute I didn't have to fight other women; in fact I'm still fighting them. Duma loves me and it's his love that gives me the confidence to stick around and put these women in their place. Don't ever doubt Edward's love for you because love you, he does. You heard the other ladies commenting this weekend about how they've never seen him so alive and happy and it's true. Edward is a catch and there are a lot of Sasas out there trying to catch him. Now is not the time to be faint-hearted. That Sasa needs to be put in her place or else she'll make your life miserable." Lulu laughed. "And kudos to you for placing her in the farthest bedroom. I bet she was quite peeved."

Sindi saw the wisdom in Lulu's words and resolved to not let Sasa affect her and to fight back. First step was to spend more quality time with Edward without Sasa around. So she asked Lulu to drop her off at her apartment. Then she called Edward and asked him to come over, and they spent the evening at her house. The rest of the week they spent at her apartment. However, on Friday

Edward insisted they spend the weekend at his place as he was feeling guilty leaving the 'still vulnerable' Sasa alone. Not wanting to look churlish and unreasonable Sindi relented.

***

On Sunday morning Sindi woke up first as usual. Feeling parched she went to the kitchen to get juice and to make breakfast for Edward. She was intent on finally making him the five-star breakfast he'd been begging for, for so long. Cooking was a big passion of hers and holding back on cooking for him had been her way of holding back giving too much of herself to him. But now she felt she was ready to share all of herself with him. When she walked into the kitchen she saw the Sunday gossip paper lying on the kitchen counter. As she headed for the fridge the huge bold headline caught her eye. Ice covered her heart and held it in a vice grip. She walked over to the counter to read it properly:

MOST ELIGIBLE BACHELOR IN SA, EDWARD BOATENG, FINALLY TIED DOWN

Sindi picked up the paper. On the cover was a picture of Edward and a beaming Sasa. Edward's right hand was touching his lapel, his cufflink peeping out of his jacket's sleeve. Sindi recognised the link; it was the one she'd helped Lulu choose. Sasa's left hand rested on Edward's chest. A huge unmistakable diamond engagement ring protruded from her ring finger. Confused, Sindi checked the date at the top of the newspaper. *Yep, today's date.* She double-checked it just to make sure. *Still today's date.* The vice grip tightened around her heart. Shaking, she forced herself to read the caption below the picture:

> SA's most beautiful couple, multimillionaire Edward Boateng and SA's darling model-turned-actress Sasa Dlamini, rocked up at last Saturday's premiere of—

Unable to read any more Sindi threw the paper on the counter in disgust as the ice covering her heart shattered, rupturing her heart in the process. *Last Saturday ... Last Saturday while I was in Hermanus. I can't believe he would do this to me! How could he get engaged behind my back?* Automatic pilot kicked in; Sindi snatched the paper up and went to the bedroom. Edward was still sound asleep. Quietly Sindi packed all her belongings and placed the paper and his sister's car key on her pillow and left. She was determined not to cry, well not until she got home anyway. She left the penthouse silently, intent on going home. Instead she was somehow found herself standing at the door to Lulu and Duma's apartment. She opened her mouth and huge sobs spewed out. Without any questions a sleepy Lulu wrapped her arms around her friend and pulled her in. Duma, who'd also woken up when the doorbell rang, wheeled in Sindi's suitcase and closed the door. He went back to the bedroom leaving the two women alone. Sindi sat in Lulu's arms crying for an hour. Finally when she was all cried out Lulu was able to piece together Sindi's incomprehensible blabbing.

Sindi's phone rang for the umpteenth time. They looked at the caller ID and saw Edward's name written on the screen.

"Maybe you should talk to him," Lulu urged.

Sindi shook her head and switched off the phone.

"How about you take a nap, sweetie? I'm sure all that crying must have given you a headache," Lulu suggested, knowing better than to push.

A nap sounded good. Sindi allowed Lulu to lead her to a guest bedroom.

***

Edward cursed when Sindi cut him off again. He threw his phone on the bed, seething with anger. He flung himself on the bed and snatched the offensive newspaper once again. He reread the caption, his eyes burning holes in the picture: his blood was boiling. He wanted to punch something. No, scratch that, he wanted to punch someone. The journalist who had written this trash would be a good candidate. But he was also angry at Sindi. How could she just take all her belongings and leave like that? She hadn't even given him the chance to give his side of the story. He was sick and tired of being persecuted for other men's sins. If she wanted to leave, then fine she could leave. He wasn't willing to live like this. Every time they hit a bump or her insecurities rose to the surface she either walked out on him or threatened to. This was the last time! He was done chasing after her. If she wanted to act like a schoolgirl then so be it. He was a grown man and he needed a grown woman by his side. And now to settle that other problem … He got up and left the bedroom.

***

Later that afternoon a rested but still weary-hearted Sindi sat in Lulu's kitchen with Lulu and Duma, the now infamous newspaper article and an empty packet of Woolies cupcakes on the counter in front of them. Sindi, in all her heartbreaks, had never known such a pain. It felt as if her heart had been shattered into a million pieces and then put together with sticky tape. But not all the pieces had been found so there were gaping holes in her heart.

"I think the two of you need to talk," Duma suggested. "The least you can do is explain why you left him and give him a chance to defend himself."

"No!" Sindi said. "He will only lie to me."

"Has he ever given you reason not to trust him?"

"No … yes, when he slept with Sasa.'

"That was a one-off mistake at a time when two you were not even dating and you forgave him for that."

"Well, he will lie, that's what all men do most."

"You can't paint all men with same brush."

"I'm sorry, my friend, but I'm with Duma on this one. You need to talk to Edward. Something's not right here. Edward would never do something like this – he's too much of a gentleman."

Sindi saw red. "Damn, girl! Talk about throwing your girl under the bus! Whose side are you on? Whose friend are you really? I can understand Duma standing up for him, but you?"

Afraid of angering her more and seeing that Sindi was still too hurt to see logic and reason, Lulu backed down.

"Yours, of course. I'm sorry if I seemed to be supporting him."

"I'm sorry too for snapping at you. Let me just go home," Sindi replied, sliding off her stool.

"Are you sure you want to be alone? You can spend tonight here. Don't you have work clothes in your suitcase?"

"I do, but the thought of being in the same building as him makes my stomach turn. I mean, what if he comes here? I'm not ready to see him."

"OK, Duma and I will take you home then," Lulu said, slipping off her stool as well.

When they arrived at her flat Lulu and Duma escorted her upstairs. Duma dragged her case into her bedroom. With nothing left to do or say Lulu gave Sindi a hug.

"Please don't pull that recluse act you pulled last time.

At least check your messages and respond even if it's via text or e-mail. I worry when you go silent."

"I will, I promise."

Duma also gave her a bear hug. "I'm sorry things didn't work out between you two. I don't know what happened but you two are soulmates. Anyone who's seen the two of you together and doubts it is lying. Don't throw away something so rare; think about it and stay strong. Lulu and I love you and are here for you." He gave her an affectionate brotherly kiss on the cheek, and then he and Lulu left.

Sindi looked around her small flat. Memories of Edward dominated her space. Edward in the kitchen, Edward on the couch, Edward lying in bed watching her in the kitchen through the open shutter doors that separated the bedroom and lounge-kitchen area. Sindi couldn't handle the memories. She decided sleep was the best option. She lay on the bed and Edward's cologne assaulted her senses. Annoyed, she jumped up and angrily stripped the bed. She opened the cupboard to take out a change of linen. She was confronted by Edward's shelf, his shoes in his corner, his spare suits and shirts behind her coats. *How did this man become so entrenched in my life so soon?* For a second Sindi entertained pulling an Angela Bassett in *Waiting to Exhale*, but her good upbringing held her back from burning his belongings. Besides, she didn't have a backyard to build a fire. She emptied out her suitcase and neatly packed his things in it. Tomorrow she would call a courier company to deliver it to him. She changed the sheets and put the used linen in the washing machine ... except for his pillowcase. She wasn't ready to completely erase him from her life. Then Sindi remembered the jewellery. It was such an expensive gift she felt it was only right to return it. She placed it in the suitcase, hiding it among his clothes, and locked the case. *I'll text him the code tomorrow after arranging the courier.* By the time she had finished she was exhausted. She climbed into bed with the pillowcase that still bore his scent and cried herself to sleep.

Thirteen

In the morning when Sindi woke up her eyes were swollen. Not wanting a repeat of last time she administered the potato remedy to reduce the swelling before she left for work. By the time she arrived at the office her eyes looked close to normal. Farranah raised her eyebrows quizzically when she saw Sindi dragging the suitcase behind her. Sindi just ignored her. She headed straight for her desk and called the courier company to arrange a collection. A reminder telling her there were only three weeks till Edward's charity ball popped up on her screen. She spent the morning frantically finalising things and chasing up suppliers, entertainers and donors. She also compiled to-do lists and contacted their regular recruitment firm to arrange for casual workers. She e-mailed Edward reminding him that the video montage and the artwork for the posters, banners and brochures needed to be signed off today in order for the printer to print everything on time.

At 11am the courier company came to pick up the suitcase. After Sindi had signed it off she texted Edward and told him the code for the case. Twenty-five minutes later, she received a curt text back:

Suitcase received, thank you.

Sindi stared at the message. She felt hurt that he had sent her such an abrupt message. She didn't know what she had expected but the coldness of his message didn't sit well with her. Hot tears prickled her eyes. She got up and went to cry quietly in the ladies'. She was relieved to find it empty. After she had composed herself, she put tear drops in her eyes and retouched her eye make-up. She returned to her desk to find she had one missed call from Edward and he'd also left her a voice message. Anxiously she dialled her voicemail box. Her excitement soon dissipated as Edward's angry voice shouted at her. *"I don't know what kind of men you are used to or maybe what kind of man you take me for. I've tried to be accommodating and understanding with you but you keep on throwing insults in my face. I had hoped we could at least be amicable to one another but clearly you are not interested. That jewellery was a gift to you – I don't want it nor do I have any use for it. I'm returning it to you, sell it, give it away – I don't care. Oh and just so you know: returning a gift is great insult in African culture."*

Sindi was shocked; she hadn't meant to offend him. She was busy trying to think of how to apologise to him when an e-mail from him entered her inbox.

Dear Ms Mali

I trust all other aspects pertaining to the event referred to in the subject line are in order. I am happy with the video and artwork. Please go ahead and arrange the print run.

Please note from now on all communication should be between you and my PA Thuli Ndlovu. I've CCed her in. She is well aware of my standards and expectations. I look forward to a worthwhile event.

With regards
Edward Boateng
Chairman: Boateng Group

Sindi stared at the screen, dumbfounded. Whoa! So she was cut out of his life completely and was saddled with her worst enemy, while Sasa was still pampered and entertained. *So much for your love for me and us being soulmates as everyone seems to think. If this is soulmate love then I don't want any, thank you very much!* Sindi resolved to stick to her pact of giving up on love if things didn't work out with Edward.

***

The weeks leading to the charity ball dragged. With each passing day the apprehension at the pit of Sindi's stomach grew. She was nervous about seeing him again. But it was her event; she had to be there on the day to coordinate everything and troubleshoot, so it was inevitable she would see him. She wondered how she would react when she saw him and Sasa together. Two weeks had passed since she had broken up with Edward. Even though she had forbidden any talk of Edward after the last e-mail from him, she still cried herself to sleep every night and she still slept with his pillowcase. Every morning she had to wake up and apply potatoes to her eyes. She was sure by now she was singly keeping the local potato industry in business. Lulu had tried a number of times to bring up the topic of Edward, even going so far as to tell her she had something important to tell her. Sindi was adamant that she had no interest in talking about Edward and, no matter how important the news was, she wasn't interested. When Lulu had insisted, Sindi threatened to disown her and ever since then Lulu never brought up Edward again.

Five days till the charity ball ...

***

Sindi was going over the final guest list the temp assistant had given her and was drawing a seating chart according to Thuli's rather rude instructions. Normally she would have allowed an assistant to handle this but she wanted to ensure no mistakes were made. In fact she'd never micro-managed so much in her life. She was sure her temp staff was irritated with her. *No matter, five more days and this man will be out of my life for good.*

The thought didn't make her as happy as it should have. Instead, it saddened her more. There was such a finality looming: five more days and any chance of reconciliation would be gone forever. *Five more days for him to finally call me. Will he do it?* Her phone rang, bringing her out of her reverie with a jolt.

"Hello?" she answered.

"Hello, am I speaking to Sindi?" A soft, voice with a delicate lilt asked.

"Yes," Sindi responded trying to place the voice. It sounded familiar.

Sindi could hear the smile on the other side.

"Hello Sindi. It is I, Grace Awola. We met two months ago. My husband and I had dinner with you and Edward and my husband told you about his childhood in Sudan."

"Grace! Of course I remember you," Sindi responded, genuinely pleased. "How are you? Are you in the country?"

The other woman laughed. Her pleasure at Sindi's sincere greeting was clear.

"Yes, we arrived yesterday. We are here to attend your event: I cannot wait. Edward showered you with so many praises I know it will be a success."

"I hope so, Grace," Sindi replied. "Thank you for the well wishes."

"Do not doubt yourself. I see a great, strong and capable woman in you."

"Thank you, Grace, I appreciate your confidence in me."

"Listen to me lecturing! I was calling about our date. Remember we said we would have lunch next time I'm in the country?"

"Y-yes ... yes. O my gosh Grace, I'm sorry but with only a few days left till the event I can only grab quick lunches."

"No problem, I understand. How about drink after work? We can just sit and have girl talk."

"Sure. I will call you just before I knock off at 5pm, and then we can decide where to meet?"

"Perfect. I look forward to seeing you."

"Me too, bye."

***

Sindi was already seated and enjoying a glass of cold Chardonnay by the time Grace arrived at the restaurant. Sindi watched the smiling older woman approach her. Sindi stood up and the two ladies hugged. Grace sat in the chair next to Sindi's. A waiter appeared immediately and Grace ordered an iced tea.

"Thank you for making time to see me," Grace said, her warmth radiating.

"It's a pleasure. Anyway, it's not like I had anything better to do."

"Oh? A young beautiful woman like you? You should have swarm of suitors beating down your door." Although it was a statement, Grace's voice implied a question.

Sindi got the uncomfortable feeling Grace was sussing her out.

"No, unfortunately not."

"No? Is it because you are not interested or are you waiting for that special one?"

"Definitely not interested," Sindi said with more emphasis than she intended.

Grace's head jerked in surprise.

"If you don't mind me saying so, you seem awfully young to feel like that. How old are you?"

"I'm 27, going on 28," Sindi answered.

Grace smiled her warm smile.

"Aah … yes you are still too young to make such a decision."

The waiter returned with Grace's iced tea and Sindi poured herself another glass of wine.

"Thank you," Grace said to the waiter. Grace changed the subject, and they spoke of other things. Soon Grace had turned the conversation back to Sindi's personal life. She had a knack of getting Sindi to open up. Sindi had the feeling that she had somehow passed some approval test. Grace looked at her watch.

"Oh my, look at the time. I am sorry I have to go. Hermann and I have a dinner engagement with some old friends."

Grace signalled to the waiter; Sindi protested.

"Oh no, my dear, I asked you out so it's on me."

"Thank you," Sindi said as Grace paid. Sindi stood up to bid Grace farewell.

Grace touched Sindi's arm lightly.

"You know, my dear, with love, you always have to be brave and you constantly take great leaps of faith. Leaps of faith are never easy or safe but the rewards are more than worth it. And sometimes, in life, we have to deeply examine even the most conclusive facts for they could have been misrepresented and misunderstood. We also need to know when to put aside our pride. You are beautiful and intelligent. Don't give up on love. True love does exist and often it is staring us right in the eye, but we miss it because we too busy focusing on other things like our insecurities and our misguided wants and fears."

With another warm smile Grace left her.

Sindi sat down and poured herself her last glass of wine. She felt Grace was trying to tell her something and she also had the feeling the reason Grace had asked her for drinks was so that she could tell her what she had just told her. Sindi began thinking about Edward and what Grace had just said to her. Annoyed with herself for thinking about Edward, she cut the thought short, placed her near-full glass of wine on the table with a small bang and went home.

***

Guests danced as the live band played. Everything had gone smoothly so far: the speeches from distinguished guest speakers, the video montage, testaments from former children of war and human trafficking and a top-notch five-course meal. Best of all was the fact they had managed to sell all the tables. Sindi hoped the auction would be just as successful. She had managed to acquire nice pieces. The pièce de résistance was a Picasso original that had been donated by a German couple she had been introduced to by her art dealer friend. She knew with this crowd they could fetch a very good price for it. Sindi took the opportunity to go outside for some fresh air. She really needed the break.

The charity ball was being held at a beautiful wine estate in Wellington. The theme was monochrome with silver accents. The beauty of Western Cape in summer was that the sun set very late so earlier in the evening guests had had the fortune of valley views from the ballroom. Seating areas had also been set on the expansive lawn. Fairy lights and lanterns had been strung around for when the sun eventually set.

Sindi spotted a bench under a big tree, some distance away from the party, which overlooked a huge pond. It had taken all her strength to not throw herself at Edward's feet and beg him to take her back. She had been watching the door, anticipating his arrival. When he walked in, his stately presence took her back to their fateful meeting in the elevator. She wasn't sure when exactly she had fallen in love with him. Some days she thought it was the moment she had first locked eyes with him and at other times she thought it was their first kiss. She was finally bold enough to admit to herself she was utterly and irrevocably in love with him. She was willing to endure a thousand Sasas and Thulis if that meant he'd be by her side. She'd been ecstatic to see that instead of Sasa he'd been accompanied by an elderly woman who she assumed was his grandmother; in fact his entire family had come to support him. Sindi had kept her eye on their table. She'd watched with a smile as his family affectionately engaged and laughed with each other. She knew that she'd enjoy being a member of his family.

She headed for the tree, daydreaming about how differently things could have been. She was so deep in thought that she didn't even hear Lulu calling out to her until she'd caught up to Sindi at the tree.

"Jeez, woman, are you deaf? I've been calling out to you."

"Sorry, friend, I was lost in thought," Sindi replied with a sad smile.

Sindi lifted the skirts of her one-shoulder black gown and sat down. Lulu followed suit with her silver off-the-shoulder gown. Both women had pinned their hair up.

"Thinking about Edward?" Lulu asked.

Tired of pretending that she was OK, Sindi looked at her friend. A huge lump formed in her throat and hot tears pooled in her eyes. Sindi nodded. Lulu shifted closer and threw one arm around her friend.

"The pair of you are driving me crazy! You're both so stubborn and your pride is hurting you. You are my friend and I love you. In public I will always have your back, whether you are right or wrong but in private I will tell you to your face when you are wrong. *Tshomi*, you were wrong so you need to make the first move and apologise to him."

"How can you say that? You saw the newspaper article."

"Yes, but your mistake was making a judgement without getting all the facts. You got so emotional you forgot to think rationally and you failed to give him a chance to defend himself."

"What was there to defend? He waited for me to go away, and then he betrayed me."

"Is that really what happened? You don't know that, you are assuming. Yes, he's not completely innocent – he should have told you he was attending the premiere with her – but you should have also allowed him to explain himself. Then you packed his stuff and sent it by courier *and* returned his gifts? Girl, that was just cold."

"I was angry at the time. I regret doing that now."

"You were too eager to find fault in him. You have to stop comparing him to the losers you've dated in the past. Judge him for who *he* is and what *he* has done, not what you anticipate."

"Maybe, but it doesn't change the fact that he did what he did."

"According to the article they went to the premiere as a couple and they were already engaged?"

"Yeah, so?"

"And we returned the following day and you asked him over and the two of you spent that whole week together living at your place while she was alone at his place?"

"What are you getting at?"

"So tell me what woman would get engaged and then allow her fiancé to leave her the following day to spend a whole week with another woman. Then he and this woman come back, get all cosy in front of her and he brazenly spends the night with the other woman while she's under the same roof? You've lived with Sasa for a few weeks – do you honestly think she would allow such a scenario?"

Sindi thought about what Lulu had just said and realised what a fool she had been by jumping to conclusions. *I should have listened to everyone; they all told me to allow him to defend himself.*

"I've been a fool and it's too late now, I've lost him."

"No you haven't. Edward is completely and utterly in love with you, and luckily for you, love means forgiveness. Trust me: he is looking for a reason to forgive you."

"How do you know?" Sindi asked sceptically.

"I live in the same building as the man, my husband is best friends with the man *and* my husband knows better than to keep secrets from me," Lulu said with typical Lulu dramatic flair. "And you didn't hear this from me but his mum was asking me about you. It seems Mr Boateng blabbed to lil' bro about you, lil' bro blabbed to lil' sis who blabbed to the parentals who blabbed to the grandparents. And, my friend, the family likes what they've seen so far."

Laughing, Sindi hugged her and jumped up. Then a thought crossed her mind.

"Wait, what about Sasa? She was wearing a ring. Is she engaged to someone else?"

"What?" Lulu gave her a 'where have you been' look. "You mean you don't know?" She yanked Sindi back down. "Edward tossed her out *immediately* after you left. He was *beyond* furious with her. You know the ring she was wearing in the pic? Well, he'd bought that ring for *you*. Sasa claimed that she saw it, tried it on, and then it wouldn't come off and she forgot about it." Lulu rolled her eyes. "As if. The journalist who wrote the story is her friend and I bet she slipped the ring on just before the picture was taken. There's no way Edward wouldn't have noticed it. Anyway, Edward had had enough of her, and long story short it turns out she had lied about having an addiction problem and about the miscarriage. Truth is, life in L.A. was hard for her. She wasn't the hot commodity over there that she had been here and she wasn't landing any jobs. Money was tight and girlfriend was used to the good life, thanks to Mr Boateng, so she lured him to L.A. to seduce him. When Edward told her about being in love with you she devised a plan to get rid of you and resume her old place. And, oh, turns out the reason she'd dumped Edward two years ago was because he had *refused* to marry her ...' Lulu stopped speaking and looked at Sindi. "Helloooo, are you listening to me?"

Sindi had stopped listening the moment she'd heard Lulu say Edward had planned to propose to her. She felt so foolish that she'd been so quick to misjudge him. She thought of the unnecessary heartache she had caused them both, all because she hadn't trusted his love for her and she'd been busy looking for clues and signs that he was another frog. Suddenly, she remembered Grace's words to her; now everything made sense. She could even understand Edward's anger towards her. Sindi jumped up again, gathered her skirts and ran towards the party.

"Sorry, *tshomi*, this is more important," she threw over her shoulder.

Sindi ran into the ballroom and scanned it for Edward. Finally she spotted him dancing with his mother. Sindi hesitated. She didn't want to be rude and disturb them and she wasn't sure how he would respond to her. She remembered Grace's words that love requires one to be brave and take leaps of faith. Also, Lulu had told her Edward's family approved of her. Sindi decided to chance annoying his mother by interrupting their dance.

She reached Edward just as the song was nearing the end. Her heart thudded against her ribcage, her throat felt constricted and her hands were shaking. Edward's mum spotted Sindi first and smiled at her, boosting Sindi's confidence. Edward turned to see who his mother was smiling at and he and his mother stopped dancing. Sindi smiled nervously at them.

"Hello, mama," she greeted politely, her manners kicking in.

"Hello, my child."

"How are you, mama?"

"I'm well thank you," Edward's mother answered with a naughty grin on her face.

Sindi could feel the rest of the Boateng clan's curious eyes watching the scene. Edward stood rigidly, his face giving away nothing.

Sindi twitched nervously. "I'm Sindiswa Mali, ma, and I was hoping to steal your son for a minute."

"Felicia Boateng, and I don't mind – he's all yours!" Edward's mother said, pushing him towards Sindi. Edward reached down to kiss his mother before she left to join the rest of her family at their table.

A new song started up. Edward took Sindi into his arms and began to sway her.

"Hi," she said nervously.

"Hi," he responded.

"Can we go somewhere and talk?"

Edward was enjoying holding her in his arms and wasn't ready to let go of her yet.

"Let's first finish this dance."

Sindi exhaled in relief; he hadn't rejected her. Their bodies swayed together. They got so lost savouring the feel and smell of the other that neither heard the band finish playing, so they were surprised to hear the auctioneer announce the auction was going to start in thirty minutes. They stopped dancing, both feeling a little embarrassed.

"Lead the way," Edward said gesturing the way.

Sindi weaved her way through the ballroom. Night had fallen and the lanterns had been lit. She saw the tree she and Lulu had been sitting under earlier was unoccupied and she headed towards it. Edward followed her.

"So ... how have you been?" she started after they sat down.

"Well thanks. You?"

Sindi closed her eyes and took a deep breath. *It's now or never.* She turned to look him in the eye. *Be brave; take that leap.* She took his hand in hers. Her heart rejoiced when his fingers curled around her hand.

"Not so well. I've been miserable without you. I love you and I'm sorry I didn't trust you – I didn't trust us. I was so busy trying to protect my heart that I neglected to appreciate the love you were giving me. My fears and insecurities led me to see what I wanted to see and I'm sincerely sorry. I can only hope that you will find it in your heart to give me another chance." Sindi chewed her bottom lip nervously, waiting for Edward to say something. Tears threatened her eyes. When he didn't say anything she said shakily, "A wise woman advised me that it takes bravery to love someone and love has no place for pride. So this is me being brave and putting my pride to the side." She laughed nervously, still waiting for Edward to respond.

After what seemed an eternity Edward grabbed her chin. He kissed the single stray tear that ran down her face and engulfed her in a tight embrace. Sindi closed her eyes and breathed his scent in, her tears flowing freely now. Being in his arms felt like returning home after years of isolation. It reminded her of how much she had missed him and how happy and safe she always felt in his arms.

"You are like home to me," he breathed into her neck, echoing her thoughts. "It wouldn't be fair for me to let you take all the blame. I contributed to our problems. I'm the one who brought Sasa into our lives. A wise man married to a wise woman told me love also means acknowledging your own mistakes."

They both laughed.

Edward kissed her full on the mouth. He broke the kiss and rested his forehead against hers. His big hands cradled her face. "I love you too. These past three weeks have been the worst in my life. It felt like the most important part of me was missing. I couldn't stand my house; it's like your presence is etched everywhere. Let's make a pact: to always be honest about our feelings, to never allow another person to enter our personal space, to always try to solve our problems without running away and to always give each other the benefit of the doubt and the chance to defend ourselves."

"Deal," Sindi agreed eagerly. She brought his face down for another kiss. Again he broke the kiss.

"Wait, there's one more thing."

"What?" she asked impatiently, eager to kiss him again.

Edward slid down to one knee. Sindi's heart jumped to her throat.

"Baby, I don't have a ring right now but these past few weeks have proved what I've known for a while now. You are my soulmate. Without you my world is dark and lacklustre. Life without you has proved to be unbearable. You are the only woman whose children I've ever wanted to father, the only woman I've ever wanted to grow old with. You inspire me to want to be a better man. I want to be the man who protects you, wipes away your tears, puts a smile on your face and in whose arms you lie in every night. Will you marry me?"

Tears streamed down Sindi's face. Emotion rendered her speechless and all she could do was bob her head like a nodding doll. A beaming Edward squeezed her so tightly she thought she was going to pop. Pulling her up with him he said, "Come meet your new family."

ANKARA PRESS
A New Kind of Romance

We hope you enjoyed reading this book. It was brought to you by Ankara Press, an imprint of Cassava Republic Press. The more you support us, the more contemporary African romance goodness we can produce for you. Here's how you can help:

1. Recommend it
Don't keep the enjoyment of this book to yourself; tell everyone you know. Spread the word to your friends and family.

2. Join the conversation
With Twitter, Facebook, blogs and even our own website, writing a review of a book you love has never been so easy. Start a conversation about the book via your own social networking site, or discuss it with others on Goodreads.com. And don't forget to leave a comment on www.ankarapress.com.

3. Buy your own copy
Encourage your friends to buy their own copy directly from our website (rather than illegally downloading it) as copies are available with special deals and discounts for them to enjoy. Your direct purchase will enable us to continue to produce the steamy stories you just can't get enough of. Support the publishers, not the pirates!

4. Read our other racy romances
We've more where this book came from and we promise that you won't be disappointed. In fact, we know that you'll be excited at having discovered our books. Browse and buy at www.ankarapress.com.

5. Consider writing your own
Have you ever thought about writing? Do you think you can compose a compelling African romance that will leave the reader hungry for more?

Then consider becoming one of our romance writers. Just follow our submission guidelines on www.ankarapress.com. We look forward to hearing from you!

Lastly, follow us on Twitter: @ankarapress, and like us on Facebook: www.facebook.com/ankarapressbooks.

www.ankarapress.com

About Amina Thula

When Amina was six years old her older brother bought her a comic book, a simple gift that would be the start to a lifelong love of books and reading. Her introduction to romance was the love triangle between comic book characters Archie Andrews, Betty and Veronica, before she graduated to the Sweet Valley and Sweet Dreams series in her teens - the start of her love affair with tall and brooding hot, dark, handsome strangers. Her first novel with Ankara Press is *The Elevator Kiss*.